# The Inventor

Jakov Lind

# THE INVENTOR

GEORGE BRAZILLER NEW YORK

Published in the United States in 1988 by *George Braziller, Inc.*

First published in Great Britain in 1987 by Methuen London, Ltd.

For information address the publisher:
George Braziller, Inc.
60 Madison Avenue
New York, NY 10010

Library of Congress Cataloging-in-Publication Data

Lind, Jakov, 1927–
    The inventor.

    I. Title.
PR6062.I45I6   1988   833'.914   88-16696
ISBN 0-8076-1203-0

Manufactured in the United States of America
by RAY FRIEMAN & COMPANY

First Printing.

For my son Simon
who went ahead of us
far too fast

I am indebted to a number of friends
who allowed me to continue my work
at a time I needed their help.
Elaine Attias, Oscar Bronner, Stanley Cohen,
Fred Jordan, Yona Nadelman-Kuenstler
and last not least
the Deutsche Literatur Fond, Darmstadt.
I want to thank them here and also
acknowledge the invaluable assistance
of Geoffrey Strachan, my Editor,
for reading and correcting the manuscript
and making useful suggestions on how to improve it.
My thanks are also due to my friend
Rachel Chodorov, New York.

Jakov Lind

*London, May 1988*

There is no being
not even the lowliest
which may not serve as a prison
for the sparks of the banished souls
seeking restoration from their exile.

R. Hayyim Vital

# Letter from Emmanuel Borovsky
## to his brother Boris Borovsky

Hotel Palace
George Town
Grand Cayman Island
10th March

If I haven't vanished from this earth altogether, dear Boris, I have reached its outer rim from where it's but a small step to enter the void. This must be the last and final station before the end of all journeys. As grim as all that? No, worse. Much, much worse. The Cayman Islands, on the map a mere inch south of Cuba, protrude from the ocean like the green fingernail of a drowned giant and this thin sliver and last semblance of a decomposed organism teems with millions of biped larvae, minute helpless wriggling creatures all gasping for air, for survival. How I got myself into this is soon explained; how I'll ever extricate myself from my marine nightmare is beyond comprehension so far.

Two things, seemingly unrelated (but are they?) cast me into this godforsaken exile. One, an unexpected change of management at the Hotel George Cinq in Paris where I had kept a cheap *pied-à-terre*, as long as my friend Charles de Tour was in charge of the establishment; the second, a not so unexpected phone call from my accountant, Joseph Samuel, instructing me to purchase a trading company in this tax-free haven with what was left in my account.

And here I am facing the blue sea and lofty green palms, a melancholic outlook I prefer to the depressing sight of the

Palace covered by black and green mould. Everything else, too, is quite disgusting here: not just the room, the food and the staff's dirty white uniforms. Even the name of my 'company', BRUSTKOPF LTD, makes me feel sick.

Today is only Tuesday: I have only been here for one week. Tomorrow at 11 am I am going to see Dudley Windermere, the manager at my local branch of the National Westminster. Maybe I can mortgage the company, trade it in for a ticket to New York. I'd do anything and go anywhere to get out of here. I have a friend in New York, Irving Cohen, a brilliant investment lawyer. His business is to buy companies; mine is to write letters and think up fabulous new and complicated projects, to brood over a sensational new invention. To own a company entitles me 'to invite finance for the development, manufacture and marketing' of my new creation. Not bad.

Thursday

I still can't quite believe it. What a disaster! Brustkopf Ltd isn't worth the printer's ink on twelve sheets of paper studded with such illustrious preliminaries as 'henceforth' and 'forthwith' to make this bit of useless document sound important. Briefly: the founders, Jacob Brustbein and Zaddik Kopfman, two enterprising Poles, managed to get away to Caracas just in time. They could have lost a real arm and a leg as well. Brustkopf Ltd bred alligators, but instead of buying young gators you can feed on leftovers, they bought mature green monsters that each needed a sheep or a goat per day. Instead of putting them in a swamp, they kept them in a swimming pool. The males began to fight and kill one another, but worse, because the management were waiting for maximum yields, the hides after a certain age became porous and brittle as old peeling wallpaper. Even the meat, a delicacy certain French and German gourmets relish, had become inedible, rotten in fact. Six hundred alligators down to the fishes. You'd think two gentlemen from Lodz would have had more sense. That was the end of Brustkopf Ltd, the company I purchased with my last bit of capital. I could tell, from the way Windermere looked at me, that he had lost all respect for people of Polish origin. Call it prejudice but I can't get a penny out of Windermere.

Sunday

Thinking. Thinking about money. Ferenczi believed money derived from 'the infantile impulse to play with feces', sublimated by 'the impingement on this play impulse of a repudiation of feces' which he connects with the development of the upright posture. 'Money is nothing other than dehydrated filth that has been made to shine. *Pecunia non olet*. Money doesn't stink.

Marx talked of money's 'mystical, fetishist character', a commodity which surrounds itself 'with the qualities of the occult'.

Freud, when he speaks of 'the end of this flight of human fancy, the end of the alchemical delusion' foreshadows 'the discovery of what things really are worth and the return of the priceless to the worthless'.

I agree with all of them. Money and, for that matter, all the values we purchase with it, is an odourless image on a computer screen, an ultimate optical illusion a mere *symbol* of reward for an instinctual need to expand mental and physical energy, a process known as LABOUR. All work creates surplus wealth and creates it in such abundant quantities that nothing except a number on a screen can encompass its total true 'value'. Money is both an electronic impulse and a matter of mathematical and philosophical speculation. Add, calculate and compute all the world's raw materials present and future, the cost of labour, production and distribution, and our life will be ruled by computed, self-evident reason. The world's *ultimate* redemption depends on such a super computer. The Redemption Machine replaces the Messiah and is about to take over . . . alas, is not about to take over the world, just the world in my head. In my present situation, I've no choice but to go back to my old vocation.

My battery-powered fountain pen, my electrical scissors, my motorized shoes, my radio hat and all the other gadgets I used to toy with, which cost me all my time and all my savings, were mere child's play. My Redemption Machine is a major project, might take as long as five years to complete, and will require major investments. To start with, as you know, I need investors who believe in me, not necessarily in my invention. To begin with I must convince myself I've reached the end of the road. Ultimately, irrevocably. Redemption from my own predicament . . . I cannot expect from any quarters unless it starts in my own brain. And that, dear brother, should explain this lengthy letter. I have discovered the germ of an idea for linking my personal fate with that of the family of men. The solving of my material problems now depends on the redemption of all mankind, and whenever a universal concern touches our private life and vice versa, new energy, new hope and renewed confidence is born. I trust you, too, will wish to purchase a reasonable share in this, my new enterprise.

Again it's Tuesday. I still can't post this letter, I don't know why. Is it that I fear you'll turn down my last request for money? No, not really.

I know you are both rich and generous. You went to university, studied, worked hard, finished the course and practised the old Jewish magic. Medicine pays. You could save. You have money left to invest. You still collect presents from wealthy patients, still get film stars and pop stars and royalty to swallow your medicine. You continue to prescribe diets to charm wealthy widows. You still buy and sell real estate through discreet agents. There are so many ways to make money for doctors, while for footloose freelances like myself there was and is only one way to survive: to invent and keep on inventing new mechanical devices, which, even if they never quite work, allow an inventor to keep working. I was about to retire in Paris when I was suddenly woken up and flung back into the harsh discipline of an exercise yard. They call it 'real life'. And here I am.

'Real life' carries me on its crest or will drown me.

I have made friends with a big, fat lady, dark and appetizing like a chocolate cake. She cleans my room, brings me food from home, talks to me about her life and reads my future in the palm of my hand. She is barely forty-six, has seven or eight children, no husband, old and sick parents and takes care of all of them. I am sure she loves me and it's mutual – but I doubt if we shall ever be lovers. She comes singing down the path with brushes and bucket and an armful of linen. I jump out of bed when I hear her coming. Within two seconds I am dressed. While I wash she takes my breakfast from the bucket. Hot black coffee, white sliced bread, cream cheese and jam. The breakfast she collects from the kitchen. Warm meals she prepares for me at home. Rice, plantains, chicken or fish and beans and sweet potatoes. It all tastes good and saves me going to the res-taurant. The hotel food is bad and expensive. Australia Mal-lone makes gourmet meals for me for one American dollar, cleans the dishes in my basin and tells me stories, most of them funny. After two weeks with Australia I am no longer so desper-ate and depressed. Australia looks after me. 'You need someone to look after you, so you can be free to do your thinking.'

I can't help loving her, that's obvious. In fact, I worship her and have all the time left to think and write and get drunk on 'Cool Jennies', the house speciality (coconut milk mixed with rum and fresh mint). 'There is a time for everything', as it says in Ecclesiastes, and now it's time to think, to imagine, to daydream.

A phone call for me from New York, from Irving. He insists that I should take a plane right away and meet him at the Palma Yacht Club at noon on Friday for lunch with the King and Queen of Spain and some of their close friends on board the Fortuna Mare II, the Royal Yacht. Needless to say I arrive at five minutes to twelve only to find that Irving had beaten me to it by ten minutes.

What a lunch! It is the first time I have seen Irving in action. He starts with Maimonedes over cocktails before lunch and while the *tapas* are being served he has already reached the expulsion under Ferdinand and Isabella. While the soup is served he talks about the return of two million Jews to Spain and by the time we reach the first fish course he is suggesting with a broad smile that the time might have come to turn the cathedral of Palma back into the great synagogue it had been before the mob razed it in 1395. 1995 would be the proper date after six hundred years to reinaugurate the Palma Synagogue on its original site, 'a correct and noble gesture, a simple act of decency, a lofty example to the rest of the world'. When we come to the meats he has his audience in tow, proposes the re-establishment of Rabbinical seminaries in Toledo and Cordova and toasts a new school for cabbalists in Gerona, which was a centre of esoteric studies back in the twelfth century. And when it finally comes to dessert, coffee, cigars and cognac Irving introduces his dumbfounded audience to the *barbarusi*, the deer-pig with two stomachs that chews the cud, the kosher pig, only very recently discovered in the highlands of Sumatra.

'We can breed it commercially in the higher altitudes of the Sierra Madre, where the climate is just right.' His Majesty and the Queen and everyone else at the table laugh out loud. 'To eat its flesh is to imbibe some of its superior intelligence,' I can hear him say with barely a grin on his chubby face, 'but there is more to eating pig than primordial ritual and certainly more to it than the simple economics of profitable livestock! The pig in fact is our Master! It teaches us to be content with such basic pleasures as eating and defecating despite our superior intelligence! The pig, alone among all God's creatures, knows the temporality of life's short existence by instinct, by heart, *because* until the very end of its life it continues to enjoy life with undiminished pleasure and ultimately sacrifices itself to our need for its flesh, so we may live and grow fat on its demise. What a spiritual lesson in humility!

'The law of Moses forbids us the animal that does not chew the cud though it may have cloven hooves. Neither Muslim nor Jew is allowed to touch it, nor did Jesus and his disciples. For

16

thousands of years Christian, Jew and Muslim cannot share the same table, then suddenly the messenger of a new millenium appears, bringing tidings on swift tall legs! Is it not a symbol of an imminent perousia when a pig comes running on the legs of a deer? What more convincing evidence of the brotherhood of men can we think of than a Holy Communion of kosher suckling pig in which Jew, Muslim and Christian can participate?

'Breeding the *barbarusi* in the Sierra Madre,' he concludes, 'completes Spain's specific universal Iberian-Christian mission to the world!'

Everyone at the table giggles, smiles and roars with laughter. 'The only way to make them listen to my plea for the restitution of Jewish capital and property after six hundred years, is to make it all sound like Jewish jokes. Everyone likes Jewish jokes, as you will have noticed,' he whispers in my ear. 'I have made us new friends. You can now approach them with your new scheme.'

True enough. It now looks as if my first investor may well be His Majesty Juan Carlos, King of Spain. On the way to the airport in the taxi, Irving suggests that I should meet a man known as Elim Ffinger, the Messiah from Antwerp. He gives me his address and promises to phone him first.

All this happens within less than half an hour, on an upright chair in front of my bungalow, while Australia makes my bed, washes my floor and tells me the story of her first lover who proposed to her on her twelfth birthday. I can't remember a word of it. My mind is on the luncheon in Palma and I try to figure out who the Messiah from Antwerp, Elim Ffinger, may be.

Yours, Manny

# Letter from Boris Borovsky
# to his brother Emmanuel

The Lodge
Bishop's Avenue
London
30th March

What, still on the road? At your age? Others at your stage in life would have retired long ago into the arms of a sweet woman, would sleep in peace, dine in style and eat healthy foods, read books and walk and swim for exercise. Natural progressions you never followed, it seems. You are still running like a white mouse in a wheel, dear brother, never weary of producing new fantasies.

Since last we communicated I have married a beautiful woman, half Jewish, half Eskimo, who was born in Siberia and is called Oksana Lieblich. She comes from a family of actors and bearhunters and grew up in a Siberian Hunters' Collective, believing in Shamans and secret spells, magic potions, spirits, demons and ghosts. The most Jewish thing about her was her father's name, Lieblich. Now, having married, she has lost even this last trapping of civility and is all foul-mouthed Eskimo bearhunter. I love her all the same and we are happy, as far as this peculiar condition of smug content can be defined.

Happy. Happy. Frankly, when I hear the word happy I feel like throwing up. But Oksana, my tough companion, says: 'You are focking happy, basta! And now shut up!' You know me. I am mild mannered when dealing with women, because (as all wise men should be) I am afraid of their tricks. And in my special situation: living with a woman who has learned how to tear a bear limb from limb, I am understandably a little more than considerate. I say: 'All right, I am happy. If you say so, I am happy.' They don't understand irony where she comes from. Of course we live like a pious couple of pigeons under the same roof: she cares for me and I care for her and everything looks perfect. I never think about my dozens of sexual conquests, scores of girlfriends, handmaidens, my four wives and various fiancées and all the other women who have crossed my path. When I say I never think of them I mean I never think of them but with the greatest of pleasure and without any malice or regret.

Maybe my witch Oksana is right and I am, God forbid, really happily married to her? When I look up from my pillow I can detect no clouds on the canopy of heavenly marital bliss that spans our four-poster shrine of love. We still spend more time in than out of bed and this after nearly two years! What do you make of that? Well, there are small clouds, of course, but most of them drift away. There is one cloud that has not moved, however. Every doctor we have consulted so far has confirmed my diagnosis. There is no reason why Oksana, just turned thirty-eight, shouldn't conceive. She just doesn't. It is not for lack of trying. We are at it all the time. We never stop. (Maybe we should give it a rest?) There is nothing wrong with her, nothing wrong with me. I have grown children, I am not anxious for new offspring, I don't have to prove anything.

After receiving no help in Harley Street or at the London Clinic, we have been to see Federbusch, a German postman on the Dutch border; we have flown to Bombay to consult a homoeopath, who gave her Royal Jelly and told her to follow a vegetarian diet; we have travelled to Seoul to meet the grand master of acupuncture, Master Kim II Sung. When you have paid enough for your optimism you either run out of money or patience. It looked as if we were wasting both and so fast that we came back to London – and now there is more trouble than ever before. Now she has decided that as she won't have a child she wants a dog.

I watch her playing with dogs. Every bloody four-footed shit-machine up and down the street has suddenly become her best friend. I feel like poisoning them with strychnine-laced sausage, the lot of them, the cats in the street as well, while I am at it. I know. I can tell. If I deny her a dog much longer she will want a cat, and frankly I would much rather be attacked by a four-footed barking mongrel I can fight back, than snarled and pissed at by one of those slick feline furry monsters on seven legs that stink up the house and land on your face while you are asleep.

Come to think of it, I can't make up my mind which I would detest more, a canine or a feline house guest. Oksana curses me in her Eskimo-Siberian dialect and, without knowing what she is saying, I can tell her words augur no good for my health. During the cold winter months she was knitting little bellywarmers for dogs; she even sold them to our local pet shop. But now that spring has come she wants to have either a terrier or a poodle. All dogs make me nervous, terriers or poodles, St Bernards or Pekinese, but in the end I can tell she will get her way and one day I'll come home and find a mongrel in the place where I usually sleep.

I am afraid of having a dog in the house. I don't know how to explain to her that dogs are unclean, more unclean even than pigs. She tells me that dogs' tongues are even cleaner than ours, even after they have put their noses in excrement. Dogs' antibodies against virus and bacteria are so dominant in fact (so Oksana claims) that kissing a dog's lips or even a tongue-kiss with a dog is tantamount to inoculation against all sorts of diseases. Who would have the strength to argue with her Siberian fairy tales? If I say, 'Let's ask a vet whether a dog's tongue is as clean as that,' she says: 'Vets, like psychiatrists, are all quacks. May they die of rabies. In Myrnyy, where I come from,' she goes on, 'we used to feed our sledgedogs with the carcasses of reindeer and their rears still smelled sweeter than our Comrade Vet's breath through his false gold teeth.'

As you may easily appreciate, a certain dread hangs over me. I hardly dare to leave the house for more than a few hours. I'm afraid she'll move in a dog or a cat. Oksana clearly needs a child. I am not a child. That's what she thinks.

Enough about me and my marital affairs. I have bought this beautiful mansion on Bishop's Avenue standing in its own grounds. We have twelve bedrooms and use only one of them. You could be staying with us, you could have an entire floor to yourself, you wouldn't be in my way, I'd be happy to have you here. 'Happy' is an exaggeration but you know what I mean. You are welcome to share my home. You could live like a *mensch* instead of the flighty existence of the *luftmensch* you seem to prefer. When you were sixteen, I remember it as if it were yesterday, and Masha Kapulsky, our headmistress, asked you what you wanted to be after you finished school, you looked at her as if she had insulted you. 'What do I want to be? I don't want to be anything,' you said. 'I am an inventor.' And when she asked you what you had invented you said, 'I invented the air!' A good answer and more true than you ever thought. Your Redemption Machine seems to be made from the same stuff.

All messianism, mechanical or not, is made of hot air. The communists in Russia give us a taste of messianism! A little imbalance now is preferable to the imbalance of Utopia. It allows for hope. Your kind of pragmatism makes me as nervous as Oksana's blind love for tail-wagging domestic animals. She, too, can only talk of 'giving love to the poor creatures', meanwhile she is ready to imprison an innocent animal, which was born to be free, behind tender heartstrings as solid as prison bars. More blood has been spilled for the sake of so-called social justice than (even) for self-preservation.

A universal and central economic barometer is not as bizarre as it may sound; your idea that you can save the world with it is silly nonsense, of course. But as long as it keeps you alive, as you yourself suggest, it makes sense. All other redemption is rubbish. As your brother who can afford it, I enclose a cheque for two thousand pounds. It should keep you and Australia and her children for a while and there might even be enough to get you out from there and back to Paris, if that's what you want.

Yours, Boris

# Letter from Emmanuel Borovsky
## to his brother Boris

Hotel Palace
George Town
Grand Cayman Island
12th April

Life is filled with miracles, every day a new one. Three days ago
your cheque arrived, for which many thanks. Now you even
have a substantial share in my new company. You are my new
partner in Brustkopf Ltd. Congratulations! Then, two days
ago, how I still don't know, I got a phone call from Antwerp.
Elim Ffinger wants me to meet him, in Reykjavik, not in
Antwerp. He had heard of me through Irving Cohen in New
York. (I am baffled as to how he could have heard from him
where I am: I can't remember ever having sent Irving a change
of address.) It's a bit confusing, even a little mysterious. But I
did receive this call to go to Iceland; he'd even refund me my
fare. So I must go, to meet a man both Irving and my friend in
Vienna Dr Armin Reichmanovsky had wanted me to meet a
long time ago. 'Crazy as a fox, shrewd as a rat and pompous as a
peacock,' Irving had described him to me.

Armin had met Elim in Rome, spent many evenings with
him. He knows him quite well, speaks of him with much
respect, even with barely concealed admiration. According to
Armin, Ffinger is a man in his mid-fifties who knows fourteen
languages, was born Samuel Butterfeld in Transsylvania, but
now calls himself 'Elim Ffinger' spelled with two 'f's). Came to
Antwerp after the war to go to Canada but stayed and married

25

the ugliest of Hermann Kirschzucker's three daughters. (Hermann Kirschzucker, as every child in Antwerp knows, is the diamond king of Antwerp.)

For seven or eight years Ffinger studied the cabbala on his in-laws' money and did little else; didn't produce children; entered no business; just stayed at home or visited his mentor, the illustrious Rabbi Saul Arjeh Hirschheimer, an octogenarian sage, with whom he discussed the *tsimtsum* and the *klippah* and esoteric cabbalistic matters of this kind. But unknown to his mentor and his family, Ffinger kept a secret friendship with a Turk, a Muslim who was himself secretly a Jew, belonging to the sect of apostates called DÖNMEH. His name was Ferdinand Moussa, a name you could fool anyone with. The Turk somehow managed to convince Elim that he (Elim) was the reincarnated Sabbtai Zvi, the Messiah, and had the right charisma, sublime intelligence, financial means and aristocrat's noble manners to become the Redeemer 'in our days'.

Elim, convinced by the Turk, went in and out of lunatic asylums, was in conflict with the law, accused of organizing orgies and secret burnings of prayer books and other liturgical paraphernalia. There were rumours about him having a hand in the assassination of an orthodox Rabbi who had put a curse on his head. All this sounds too interesting to let go by, besides, you never know: a Redeemer might find a Redemption Machine very useful.

I nearly broke Australia's heart when I told her I had to leave. She sobbed and cried. I had to promise I'd be back. She is right, how could I leave her? But I must go. I gave her a month's wages in advance but it isn't money that could console her. I can hardly believe that I'll soon be in Reykjavik and not sitting on the porch of my bungalow on Alligator Island – with Australia's voice in my ears.

Hotel Siguurd
Gudmundsen
Reykjavik

Sunday

It has been a complicated and tedious journey via Nassau, Miami, London and Luxembourg, and what a journey!

Yesterday we left Luxembourg at 2 pm together with forty middle-aged German ladies on board who were off to see the gushing geysers of Iceland under the guidance of a sweet-looking sex therapist, a very attractive young woman called Dr Asmus. We should have arrived at 5.30 pm. Two hundred miles south of Iceland and twenty-four thousand feet above the roaring Atlantic, one of the Dakota's four propellers packed up. Seat belts had to be fastened, hushed silence fell except for mumbling lips trying to settle last accounts with our Maker. Captain Caspar Strommer, a cool Swede, smiling and dapper as a herring, walked through the aisles assuring us of something he could not possibly believe himself – that the Dakota, the old-fashioned four-propeller model, was the world's safest aircraft – it could also perform on two and even on one engine.

If you will believe that, you can also believe in reincarnation, resurrection and anything else you care to believe in as well. The couple next to me, he in priest's and she in nun's garb, were indeed an odd couple, as couples come. It turned out that both of them were German, but Germans who left Germany immediately after the war. They also claimed to be brother and sister, the two youngest children of Bavarian peasants out of a family of fourteen. His name was Brother John and her name Sister Agnes. Before their move to St Joseph in Prescoe, county of Limerick, they had been Johann and Agnes Pohl.

The war changed more than their names. One of their brothers, Ulrich, had been one of Himmler's henchmen, a proper war criminal, who had murdered Jews, partisans and Russian prisoners of war by the thousands and was still somewhere in Paraguay living the life of a retired planter. To atone for his sins, Johann and Agnes, who truly believed they were their brother's keeper, became a monk and a nun respectively, attached to the same orphanage in Limerick.

It had been no easy decision to make. Agnes had been one of Eva Braun's best girlfriends and had spent many weekends with the Hitlers in their Berchtesgaden home, while Johann Pohl had commanded the famous submarine *Seewolf*, which sent more than twenty-four British and American merchant ships to the bottom. Framed by Doenitz for being a fellow conspirator of Canaris, he submerged under the Soroysund near Hammerfest in Norway until he could capitulate to a British destroyer.

His voice became more of a whisper as the prayers became louder. It was the opportune moment to quote Job and recite the psalms. I watched his eyes – the hard grey eyes of a seagull, totally unsuited to a Bavarian peasant's son. His eyes were fixed on the image of his Saviour in his hand and he didn't move his lips. 'Listen, my God, to my pleading. Do not hide thyself when I pray.' Psalm 55. He stroked the words with nimble fingers like a blind man reading Braille. Sister Agnes, her eyes closed in meditation, held a rosary wound around her index finger. I don't know what I was thinking any more. In fact I don't think I had anything on my mind. My mind was as empty as the late afternoon sky. I kept repeating to myself: You are dead and considering you are dead you aren't doing too badly! Now was the time to quote my favourite sentence from Job. 'The righteous and wicked are equal before God, who holds all mankind in contempt and laughs at the trial of the innocent.'

Brother John confirmed that he had heard what I had whispered with a nod of the head. Sister Agnes opened her eyes for a moment.

I know another sentence by heart and they both seemed to love the second sentence even more than the first. 'Behold, He putteth no trust in His servants and His angels He charges with folly.' I detected a faint smile on their curled lips, curled with resignation and a little disgust for the ruthlessness with which the Lord punishes those who love Him.

Then came the miracle. Thanks either to our prayers or to the engineering superiority of the old Dakota, the plane made a perfect landing. Sustained applause, tears and nervous laughter. 'Our time has not come – not yet,' said Brother John, which was the obvious observation to make. The Reykjavik fire brigade with all its twenty engines, and what looked like an entire regiment of policemen, with four ambulances in attendance, were lined up like a guard of honour when we descended the stairs.

As we entered the arrivals hall our reception was even more overwhelming. The Chief of Police and the Mayor were at hand and so was the Minister of Transport. Ground hostesses handed bunches of roses to the female passengers; we men received bottles of eau de cologne aftershave; the children were given toys, colouring pencils and sweets. Blaring music. Thundering ovations. Lengthy speeches in an English and German no one could understand. Handshakes. The exchange of phone numbers. The taxi to the hotel was paid for by Icelandic Airlines.

My hotel, the Siguurd Gudmundsen, known to its long-time American residents as the 'Ziggy', was built in 1812 and finished the day Napoleon was taken to Elba. The Emperor never set foot in Iceland. Still the ancient hostelry they created for his visit compares favourably to all the Ritzes and Claridges, Pierres and Connaughts around the globe and was not a wasted investment. Its Empire and Biedermeyer furniture; its golden-framed panels in soft yellows and whites; its high ceilings, crowded with floating nymphs, cheerful cherubs and lusty fauns; its curtains, wallpapers, carpets and flower arrangements; everything down to the polished brass of the spittoons spoke of an aristocratic Scandinavian precision which has its peculiar melancholy elegance and refinement of taste, a positive magic power that banishes all fears of death, certainly my own.

The marble walls mirrored in golden taps, under the crystal chandelier of a thickly carpeted bathroom, made me rise from inside an eternal and complete darkness, under the pack ice hundreds of fathoms below the North Atlantic, back to life. There was no doubt in my mind that I had risen from the dead. Fear must have killed me but now I could convince myself by looking in the mirror that I had actually been resurrected – and this only minutes before I was about to meet the Messiah! The ultimate and final miracle. I emerged from the bathroom smiling like a newborn babe and instantly ordered champagne and caviar from room service.

Three knocks were followed by the sound of a key being turned in an attempt to unlock the door. I froze for a moment, looked through the spyhole. No, I can't say I was physically afraid of him but maybe a little apprehensive, watching him the way one watches a horsefly. The first thing that struck me about him was that he looked strangely familiar. He was dressed 'outlandishly' for lack of a better word. I stared at him, couldn't quite believe my eyes. Here was a man I had definitely never met before, yet I knew him, knew him only too well. What I report to you here is the absolute truth, yet I can't expect you to believe me. Except for his nose, which was thinner than mine, he more or less looked like . . . myself. He had firm, strong blue eyes, the same colour and the same shape as mine, and his brown-grey tinted bushy hair was parted on the left, the way I wear it. His upper lip was as thin as mine, his lower lip a little thicker. His ears were shaped like mine, with long, loose, hanging earlobes. His neck was firm, short and strong, his torso slender, more narrow than mine, but he is also muscular, a middle-aged bull. Even the way he stood, leaning slightly back to balance his paunch, seemed identical. Then, thinking of his name, I observed his hands, especially his fingers. They were long and bony and probably triple-jointed, like the fingers of an ape, definitely not my hands and fingers. He stared back at me a little disgruntled. A schoolmaster's glance at a bright and stubborn student.

When he opened his mouth I sighed with relief. I had been afraid our voices, too, would be identical. This was fortunately not the case. He spoke with an East European accent, using a clipped Flemish syntax.

'Fiddling a lock with a key is my sense of humour. I enjoy frightening people. While I can frighten others, I am never afraid myself. Can you explain that?'

He had given himself away with these few words. I could relax. His case was beyond the simple description of mad or crazy, yet, just like his face, extremely familiar. After the first bottle of Moët et Chandon (I admit the stuff went to my head and made me feel quite drunk), I became blunt and said that I now realized I should have stayed in the Caribbean, instead of going halfway around the world to meet, at best, a future investor, and, at worst, my *doppelgaenger* – only one who sounds much weirder and seems to be much more eccentric than I could ever be. He laughed and reached me his card.

ELIM FFINGER

THE UNIVERSAL SOCIETY OF MESSIANIC PRETENDERS

PRESIDENT

He then proceeded, without my challenging him or interrupting him, to inform me that he was quite aware that I had been 'sent' to spy on him, but that he was not afraid, as he is used to meeting agents of the KGB, CIA, the Mossad, the French Secret Service, the Belgian Securité Nationale, etc etc, knowing damned well who they are and what they want from him and being quite aware that 'everyone' knows he works for the Most Superior of all Intelligence Services, the Divine Will Himself. 'One small mistake and I'll be instantly recalled and can expect neither leniency nor mercy from my patron.'

Meeting my first Messiah in an alcove of an elegant suite, close to the North Pole, where at the press of a button hot toast and caviar, herring, vodka and champagne are served by quiet, sullen-looking Moroccan waiters, I felt I had little to say and a lot to learn.

At a given moment he quoted the philosopher Edgar Wind: ' "Because the Ultimate One is invisible, his visible manifestations must be manifold. Poetic pluralism is the necessary corollary of the One, that's why the Platonists used various metaphors."'

Did he mean to say that he believed in a multitude of gods as Elim, his first name, spells? Or does it mean he believes himself to be God and is only pretending to be His agent? Instead of a clear answer he mumbled something about Pan who is 'clearly hidden in Prometheus and that's how, through the secret gate of mutability, the universal invades the particular.'

The Icelandic white nights have begun, another few weeks and the sun will not set all night. It was three-thirty in the morning, the pigeons and all other birds had started the day. Sleep had to wait and might never come. I seemed to be in the middle of a dream all the same.

He made no move to leave, as if he were still holding back something I should know. I was convinced that I had heard and seen it all by now, having realized right away that it would be a total waste of time to mention my idea of electronic redemption and the question of how and if and whether it would work. Still, now I was here I owed it to myself, if not to him, to listen until he fell off his feet or I passed out, worn out from the ordeal of a near-fatal disaster and the subsequent drinking bout. He still had a confession to make and had decided I was the man to talk to.

'I confess,' he said with a heavy tongue, 'my desire to rule the world stems from my sexual impotence. I have only once, excuse the expression, fucked my wife: on our wedding night. And never again. I can't do it. She is simply too ugly. Shall I show you a picture?' He fumbled through his pockets to find his wallet and took out a picture of a fairly soft-hearted looking dark-haired Jewish girl, neither particularly pretty nor particularly ugly, a face without any distinctive lines. Her brown eyes seemed just a little dead and her complexion a bit yellow. 'Isn't she the most ugly creature you ever saw?'

I told him frankly no, I had seen much worse. I didn't think she was either ugly or good-looking, she just looked like someone whose face one instantly forgets. 'She looks normal, like most people.'

'You don't have to sleep with her, it's easy for you to talk. Let me repeat . . .' and he repeated: 'Impotence is the cause of my messianic ambition, because real power can never be projected into the future. It either exists or not; it is always concrete reality.'

'Why do you think the Jews are waiting for a future Messiah and don't accept that Christ was the one?'

'Because we believe in the power of minorities. No Jew can be a Messiah, because as soon as he declares himself to be the Messiah, the non-Jew will try to convert him to his pagan credo, which always champions the cause of the "masses". "Masses" is a non-Jewish concept. If necessary, the non-Jew will make a God out of a teacher as the goyim did with Jesus and the communists with Lenin. That's why to be the Messiah you must not be a Jew and that's why I am not Jewish.'

'Another question. If you are not an impotent man could you not also be a woman with male genitals, to change the subject? Because after what you told me I can't take your messianic pretensions seriously. You are a Jew, aren't you?'

'A question to which I can only answer "Yes and No". But I am definitely not a woman, not as far as I can tell. Let's stop this personal inquest and remember what Edgar Wind, my teacher, says about the ineffable God. To quote Wind: "The unfolding of the divine name is multiple and always capable of increase and each single name is related to the true ineffable name as the finite is related to the infinite." '

He suddenly got up, about to leave. 'Tomorrow we'll drive out to the lake and there'll be plenty of time to continue our discussion,' he said, and left. I tossed and turned, couldn't keep my eyes closed. Whenever I shut them I saw and heard myself, I could swear, talking to myself with his voice.

Monday evening
We met at 11 am in the breakfast room. In the light of day he

seemed pleasantly jovial and normal, looking even more like myself than last night, but maybe I had got used to it. To cap it all he now claimed to be a kind of inventor as well and declared he would show me his 'model' which he keeps safely underground guarded by an elderly couple on the shore of a lake three or four hours due north of Reykjavik.

One particular seagull watching us from the windowsill as we ate looked at us out of eyes filled with a certain hatred and disgust. Its look reminded me of Brother John's on the plane when he had stared at the little statue of his Saviour in his lap. I watched Ffinger eating: he eats with his hands. I felt uncomfortable at the thought of spending time alone with this man. Please write to me in Reykjavik, keep in touch. Just in case you don't hear from me soon, you'll know where to enquire after me. Anything can still happen, I'm afraid.

Yours, M.

# Letter from Boris Borovsky
# to his brother Emmanuel

The Lodge
Bishop's Avenue
London
28th April

Being at the North Pole with a madman from Antwerp makes more sense than spending one day longer with this Siberian she-devil. I blame the Tibetan Cure, Gadogado, derived from the ovaries of a Tibetan breed of sheep reared in Switzerland. It also comes from Switzerland, this evil-reeking concoction brewed by the Dalai Lama's private physician (so it says on the pamphlet) and is supposed to be a wonder fertility drug. The effect, after three weeks of a constant period, was to turn her into a neurasthenic, hysterical wreck. Our sexual appetite has long ago trickled away with her menstrual blood. When not screaming obscenities she dozes off when we are alone in a room. Occasionally she shouts at me: 'I still love you, you bastard!' A few minutes later she threatens to kill me with a bread knife and slit her wrists afterwards. Or she throws tantrums of jealousy, accusing me of having looked at our cleaning woman's bottom when she climbed on a stepladder to clean my bookshelves.

When I want to go out she says: 'You might not find me alive when you come home!' When I lock myself up in my study she calls me a child-molester and masturbator. When I tell her to shut up, she slams all the doors and puts on every TV and radio set in the house. Full blast of course. After that we usually begin to wrestle. I am not in top form but am getting better at it. She now wears jump suits and overalls. I'll have to do the same.

O what a cholera this woman is! How can I get rid of her? Yet I love her more than ever. That's my insane fate.

I often thought of you as stark raving mad, as you well know, because of your life style, because you are trying to live out your own fantasies, a kind of Walter Mitty, a Baron Munchausen, a light-hearted, irresponsible fool. I am no longer so certain who of the two of us is which. Does my identity crisis show symptoms of latent schizophrenia? Blood pressure and heart are fine so far. But for how much longer can I take this demon?

There are so many attractive women in London in need of a man like me, a reasonable, well-mannered, educated man of independent means. Why don't I go out and find one? Because I'm a coward who believes it's heroic to suffer the insufferable, tolerate every outrage, allow her to trample all over me. Yet I used not to be this masochist when I was younger. Don't you remember how I was known as a sadist, a rough street fighter? They called me 'bandit' and 'killer' as you must know only too well, because it was you who suffered the most from my blows, without ever deserving those outbursts of my vile temper. I still regret it; that's the way it sometimes goes. The lions turn into toothless lambs. There is something extraordinarily allegorical in this unpredicted justice being meted out to me!

It was me and no one else who picked her up at a party, brought her into my home. For the first three days I didn't let her go out, guarded her like a treasure, like a wolf guards his prey. I could have loved her to death and nearly did. Then she recovered and now I am losing my strength and worst of all my sense of humour, the joy I take in a world that gets darker by the day as we grow older and so ripe that, we might soon drop off.

Yours, Boris

# Letter to Boris Borovsky
# from his brother Emmanuel

Hotel Kempinsky
Kurfürstendamm
Berlin
2nd May

Much has happened since I wrote to you last time, so much, in fact, that I hardly know where to start, so I'd better begin with Tuesday, 17th April when we left the hotel in Reykjavik in a rented Volvo.

After Droningenhuset, Boonervikken and Leifsted, the traffic faded away and now ours was the only car on the road, indeed it seemed like the only car in the whole wide world. The emptiness of the landscape was baffling. Small volcanoes and gushing geysers from hot springs rose above lava formations. Grey and black with enough small patches of green here and there to feed a few stray sheep. Emptiness, nothingness itself gradually materialized before my eyes. A picture of what 'nothing' looks like, a concrete image of the void. At last.

As we drove true north, trees appeared unexpectedly like the spread-out fingers of warning hands. How could this road possibly continue? On both sides of it were stagnant pools. The pools expanded into bogs, marshes and small lakes. Reservoirs of water set into volcanic stone. Barely a breeze. The air pleasantly tepid and humid. A chilly but fine spring day. Intermittently the sun illuminated one patch of landscape then another. I recognized whooping cranes, Queen's herons, black crows, small brown Danish seagulls and Barbarai – a rare species of flying penguin one finds only here or on the Galapagos Islands.

It was nearly two in the afternoon. We had driven for two hours without one single word spoken. When we reached the top of a slight hill we left the car to stretch our legs. Dimensions and perspectives superimposed on a map of infinity. The colours equally indefinite. Light brown. Grey-blue. Golden filigree and ashen white and yellow. Rust brown and cobalt blue. An abstract still life breathing a mild spring air.

A hundred miles or so away: a cabin and a lake. I felt I had nothing to look forward to when we finally arrived. If anything, it would be something eerie and probably unpleasant.

We drove on for many more hours through total wasteland. Not even grass, no heather. All sky and water, ridges and lines. Abstract reality, for want of a better description. Elim obviously knew where we were heading. There was no traffic and no need to keep his eyes on the road. Then, looking to the northeast, we both spotted a strange figure on the horizon. A rider on horseback who for a moment appeared above the skyline but vanished more or less instantly, leaving us to ponder all kinds of allegories.

I don't know what you do when you have to sit for hours cramped in a car seat. I ponder the meaning of words. What we had seen was a phenomenon, a thing perceptible to the senses, an apparition. The word 'phenomenon' derives from the Greek, from *phaos*, light (the Latin for it is *focus*) and the words *phantom* and *fantasy* are related to the same and so is *Hierophant*, one who shows the sacred mysteries. Looking at Elim I suddenly realized the company I was in. I had come to Iceland to find a new investor. What I had found instead was some kind of strange Master, who either gave instructions by keeping his mouth tight shut or treated me to unexpected definitions such as: 'Identity is the qualitative will of a thing to exist, no personality can be without it, yet there is an evident paradox here, because personality can exist without identity.' Or: 'You probably know the answer to this conundrum. You may presume that there can be quality without substance or, for all I know, conceive there is life after death. Who knows? It's not logical, which is not to say that it's impossible. The body dies, the anima continues. We can hear and see the dead. That's a fact, but can they see and hear us?'

'I wish you would change the subject. Let's talk about Icelandic herring and potatoes instead. This place is eerie enough as it is.'

'But the image of a dead person is often clearer than it was in their lifetime, as if an essence and not just a turbulence had survived. Often we see a face or hear a voice better when it's no longer attached to a body. Death is our future too. But what about them? Do they also see and hear us better?

'Ever heard of the Katteman Syndrome? The great Abraham Katteman, a professor at Utrecht in the late thirties, described the case of a Dutch farm worker, one Tinus Van der Bril who felt ignored and neglected by his wife. He revenged himself by teasing her for being overweight. She committed suicide.

'When she was dead he believed she would no longer ignore him. This turned out to be true. Now that he had every reason to feel guilty for her suicide, he had also become "somebody not to be ignored". All he had needed was guilt, so as to discover his identity and even some sort of self-respect. The man is still alive, incidentally, lives near Utrecht and breeds pigeons. One of them he calls Emma, after his late wife. Here you have a case where a man was more or less forced to commit murder in order to regain his lost dignity or establish a new, more charitable image of himself. That's why there is no punishment for the premeditated murder of a spouse. You can kill your wife or husband out of jealousy and in many courts you might get away with it. *"Crime passionnel"* they call it in French.

'But whether you get sent back home or locked up forever behind bars – the crime is the punishment. You have sentenced yourself to death. That's why so many wife-killers commit suicide, after a period of introspection. The death penalty is in fact the kindest sentence they can receive and they have every

reason to prefer it to be carried out by a state-appointed execu-
tioner who'll do an efficient job, rather than leave it to their own
amateurish and cowardly attempts. The Katteman Syndrome is a
nasty twist of the old onion (he pointed to his head) and I
believe it's what I'm suffering from.'

Just as there are moments when all one's senses fall apart, so
there are times when all things suddenly correlate and make
one cohesive, clear pattern. As we drove along I suddenly
believed I could see scars on his forehead and wrists, the scars
of failed suicide attempts. Now the dead eyes, or maybe just sad
eyes of that unhappy young woman also made sense, as well as
his claim of never having slept with her except once on their
wedding night. When dawn came he had either strangled her or
drowned her in the bathtub.

In spite of all my misgivings about him, I had no choice.
Whether he had killed his wife and, for all I knew, other people
as well, I couldn't just leave the car in this wilderness and walk
back. As I had noticed when he came in the other night, his very
physical presence made me feel apprehensive. For all I knew
now, he might be more dangerous than a fat horsefly and carry
the deadly sting of a tarantula concealed on his person. Not that
it made much difference in my present condition but I wondered whether Armin, who had always insisted that I should
meet his friend from Antwerp, knew what I knew now. Knew?
Even to say 'I knew' is an exaggeration. I knew nothing.

Elim Ffinger might be just an ordinary intellectual whose
mind had snapped. Nothing very unusual in that and because
he was wealthy he could indulge in such insane whims as
calling himself the President of a Universal Messianic Society
and travelling. So what? There are legions of eccentrics and
maniacs of all hues, some rich and some very rich and others
who have become princes and rulers. And what if he had killed
his wife? As long as he felt no need to confess to it I felt no desire
to make him talk about it. There are murderers everywhere and
they don't necessarily show it in their faces. You ride with them
in buses and lifts. You sit next to them on an aeroplane or at the

cinema; you stand with killers in the queue at the post office or when paying your bill at a self-service restaurant. 'The murderers in our midst' are not news, especially not to us who drifted through Poland, Austria and Germany in the years immediately after the war. Murderers, torturers, sadists all shed their uniforms like snakes their skins; they are nothing to get alarmed about.

We finally arrived at the shore of a lake which was separated from the sea by a thin strip of lava. A boat with a small outboard motor was tied to a wooden pier. We untied the rope, revved up the motor, and from there it was no more than a quarter of an hour to our final destination, a chalet on a lake with small outhouses set back from the shore.

Gretta and Gunnar, like an ancient couple of gnomes, both bent over and shrivelled up by arthritis yet with healthy complexions, welcomed us, with many gestures. They grunted and grovelled around us, took off our shoes and proceeded to undress us, made us slip into wooden shoes and gave us towels. The house spelled tidy order and smelled of wonderful foods, freshly cooked. Ice-cold aquavit, beer, titbits of herring and rye bread was the traditional welcome. We said 'skoal' and 'cheers' a dozen times, then walked to the small wooden hut at the edge of the lake.

On the short path to the sauna, as I felt the ground under my feet again after six hours on wheels, it was as if I had just stepped from an aeroplane. I breathed a lungful of Nordic silence. Nothing compares to it in purity. There were two saunas in the hut. Two small cubicles. One overheated, the other lukewarm. I wondered why two saunas should be necessary in this desolate place. I soon found out. In the cubicle which was barely warm some floor tiles covered a manhole. Green and red lights cast eerie shadows over a stainless steel box which stood on end, a six-foot high and four-foot wide 'monolith', with barely visible grooves etched into its surface. Elim stroked the grooves as if he were reading Braille. He has extremely long, well-shaped fingers but each one of them could well be double- or triple-jointed, like the fingers of an ape, with long, untrimmed nails. Strange hands.

'Let's have our sauna first; clean up, then have supper. When the old couple go off to sleep, we'll come back and you can have a better look at my baby.'

'Whatever you say.' On the way back to the house it crossed my mind that a man with such fingers might very well call himself 'Finger' and add another 'f' for emphasis.

Gretta and Gunnar brought us dish after dish, like two wound-up penguins. It made no difference to them what we said and what language we spoke in. They were both born deaf and dumb. Their eyes spoke, filled with a jubilant mood. They were overjoyed to serve their Master and his guest. An all too rare opportunity to prove themselves. The food was really excellent. They read it from my eyes and gave me large grins and chuckles, even though they didn't understand a word of my praise.

And as for what happened subsequently, dear Boris, it will try your credulity. It certainly shattered mine. While wiping the corners of his mouth, and pushing his plate away, Elim remarked: 'The holographic paradigm means that all reality is an illusion. I happen to like illusions.' Then he said something to Gunnar in rapid deaf-and-dumb language, moving his fingers before the old man's nose.

Minutes later Gunnar returned with a shaving mirror. Elim handed it to me and said in a deep, sonorous voice: 'Look at yourself. All you believe you can see now you may call recognition. You have seen yourself before and will recognize yourself. God created man in his image, now look at the image.'

I looked, and whether it was aquavit or his hypnotic voice and stare, something strange happened. Instead of seeing my own face in the mirror I saw his. Again and again I looked and again and again I saw his face in the mirror and not mine.

'A magic mirror, what? I bought it many years ago from a magician called Max Jablonski; claimed he had magicked himself out of Auschwitz with the help of this looking-glass. Don't ask me how. I never asked him. But when I met him, shortly after the war when he came to Antwerp on his way to Venezuela and needed money for his fare, he demonstrated it. Every time I looked into it, I began to see Jablonski's face. But it can do more tricks than that.'

He twizzled the knob and handed it back to me. And now, believe it or not, in the mirror was the same picture of his wife he had shown me before, but this time it moved. A TV picture. The mirror had turned into a small screen and I saw this woman, who was obviously his wife, sitting in what I believed must be their kitchen at home. She sat there, drank coffee and was engrossed in a book. Occasionally when he addressed her, she would look back at him, at us, but without speaking a word.

'But that's your wife,' I stammered.

'Well, so what? Did you think she was dead?' He had of course read my mind.

'No, no,' I lied.

'Never mind.' Then he addressed his wife and talked to her at length in a mixture of Dutch-French and Yiddish. What he said is hard to repeat: all I could make out for certain was his assurance that he loved her, loved her more than ever and would soon be back home. At the last sentence his wife looked surprised and then smiled happily. A child to whom a toy had been promised. She waved to us, yes, waved to us. She had obviously heard what he'd said. She waved and blew him kisses and then the mirror suddenly went blank. Seconds later both our faces gradually emerged slowly as if the mirror could equally serve as a photographer's dish filled to its rim with developer.

While all this was happening, the magic hands of the two kobolds had cleared the table and cleaned the kitchen. Everything was as neat and tidy as when we arrived. The small flower vase stood again in the centre of the table, with two ashtrays at either end. The trolls had taken themselves off to bed. We heard them snoring, so loudly it made the kitchen windows rattle. Elim went to a cupboard and took out a big torch, as big as a car battery. It carved a beam of brilliant light through the grey evening. It was much darker than I had expected. On the horizon there was a faint Nordic glow. A chilly breeze slapped the water. An owl screeched, like a referee's whistle, a kind of warning for the other trolls, gnomes and kobolds to retreat back into their hiding places. Humans! Beware! I swear I saw shadows of dwarfs bobbing along the water's edge, keeping their heads down. I could even see why they had to be careful. Rifle muzzles protruded from under the water's surface, emitting colourful, silent explosions.

When we finally reached the sauna Elim pressed a switch under the slanting thatched roof. The night air around us lit up with an eerie violet blue. He called it: 'An invisible light, which cannot be detected from a distance beyond fifty yards.'

We stepped back into the sauna and this time he pressed little black buttons all over the walls which gave the impression he was squashing flies. The Lord of the flies, the devil, that's him! I should have known. He is the fiend, he is about to kill me, too, and all there will be left of me is my image in his magic mirror.

Believe me, dear brother, there are moments in life when you want the worst to be over as soon as possible because the tension has become unbearable. It was one of those moments. When he asked me to stroke my finger across the warm steel, as he had done before, I hesitated, afraid at first of setting off an explosion. But then, to prove to him that my courage could defeat his black magic, I stroked the metal. Stranger things happened than a mere detonation. Through my finger, the top of my right index finger, came the scrambled sounds of a male voice. I could hear by touch, as it were, and what I heard was equally bizarre. And the voice spoke the following words:

'I believe with perfect faith in the faith of the God of truth, the God of Israel, who dwells in the *sefirah tefereth*, the 'glory of Israel', the three knots of faith which are one, that I, Samuel Abraham Butterfeld, also known as Elim Ffinger, am the true King Messiah and have come to unite and rule all creatures

44

under the sun with wisdom, equanimity and mercy, with justice, with love and with reason.'

No point in repeating here the other nine *Sacred Statements* which, according to Elim, the Redeemer has to make. They all sounded much the same to me. A lot of nonsense and I said as much. It made him furious and he gave me a long lecture to the effect that he had repeated these very words for nights and days on end and 'even in my sleep' all the way from Antwerp, yet had somehow succeeded in registering them 'without mechanical aids' over three thousand miles away!

'Fabulous, fabulous!' What else could I say to calm him down?

'You will have noticed,' he lectured me, 'no aerial, no wire, not a single knob and it's not steel either, just made to look like steel.' He knocked on the 'monolith'. It sounded hollow. I now also noticed that it was not square but oval-shaped. An elongated stainless steel egg. He kept insisting it was not made of steel but from a hard wood that grows in Surabaya, called *Surabu*. I don't know what exactly sparked off my sudden anger, but before I knew what I was saying, I shouted: 'To hell with you! Let me out of here!'

His face came closer: 'Hard as steel and my words resound from it. How much more difficult can it be to penetrate the thick skulls of the world's leaders, so that they may believe in me?'

I said, that would be hard to guess, no more, but had barely finished my sentence when I felt a short sharp pain in my forehead and skull. He saw my agony and grinned, while it seemed as if blue and white flashes, like millions of volts, were passing through him. Did the ground under my feet tremble or did I imagine that too? Cold sweat soaked my neck.

'Earthquakes and tremors are common up here. More fertile earth rises from the bottom of the ocean with every tremor. This constantly adds new magnetic energy to the virgin soil.'

He looked me straight in the eyes. Those crazed fanatical eyes I could no longer recognize as my own. My feet seemed glued to the ground. I couldn't lift them or I might have run out, maybe even jumped into the icy lake just to escape his eerie company. 'Go to hell! Let me out! Out of hell! Let me go!' I stammered.

He must have switched off some of his magnets which were probably buried under the tiles. Now I could move again. I ran out and up to the house.

He followed me, after switching off the lights in his sauna. Back at the kitchen table under the paraffin lamp everything seemed normal again. My host no longer had phosphorescent red and green sparks in his eyes. He looked his usual jovial self. He poured us coffee from a thermos flask and found a tin of Danish butter cookies. We ate and drank coffee and pretended nothing had happened.

I must have needed to meet a man such as Elim Ffinger. The longer I thought about it, the more I realized how important this encounter with a kind of *doppelgaenger* was for me. Just listening to him proved I had been wrong about my own state of mind all along. In some inexplicable way this man, so similar yet so alien, articulated my own troubled mind, preoccupied with universal solutions for my limited concerns. When I listened to him, talked to him, I felt both very depressed but also exceedingly liberated. He made me feel quite normal so to speak.

Whatever I needed to learn from this Icelandic saga I had now learned. I wanted out of there – and the sooner the better. Then . . . suddenly there was a barely audible chirp. It startled us both. He opened the door. A bird with human features (called a *Harpie* I believe) dropped a piece of paper on the doorstep and took off. It was a telegram. He read it and pulled a grave face.

'Let's pack up and go,' he said in a matter-of-fact way. 'I have to return to Antwerp.'

Dear Boris – what an unexpected relief! I got up and began to pack. Elim too disappeared into the bathroom to get ready for the journey back.

Only the deaf and dumb have a third ear. Both Gunnar and

Gretta stormed down from the attic like poltergeists, instantly put on water, began to slice bread, and set cheese, jam and butter on the table. We had a hurried breakfast. Elim had accounts to settle with them, I went ahead with the bags. The still waters reflected seals and gulls, moving clouds and little else. The stillness was overwhelming. A serene beauty beyond words; and, even though I couldn't get away fast enough, an inexplicable nostalgia for this perfect tranquillity I was about to leave overcame me.

I had to close my eyes. The light over the sea was glaring. Finally Elim emerged with quickened steps, as if in a big hurry. I started the motor, unfastened the rope and we moved away quickly. Gunnar and Gretta, as they stood there on the board-walk like two garden gnomes, wiped real or imaginary tears into their aprons and sleeves. They waved and we waved back. They shrank to small dots and were gone.

As we drove back the skies, pink-orange and purple-mauve, receded upwards and took the earth with them into a world beyond earthly concerns. On the long journey back to Reykjavik we didn't exchange a single word. We took the lift together and I noticed a brooding look, a slight movement of his lips. He was obviously not yet ready to go to sleep and stepped out of the lift on my floor, ready to join me in my room. I felt a little sorry for him but didn't want him in my room, where he might get too comfortable. So he wouldn't invade my privacy I thought it might be a good idea to fire a few personal questions for him to answer on the spot. I had guessed correctly: ask a man about his mother, when he least expects it, and he'll respond.

'Well, if you really want to know, my mother was a conceited, savage woman, very beautiful and very unhappy, also very rich. When my father left her for a younger woman on her thirtieth birthday she began to go out with all sorts of men and brought them home. A little music, a tango, a few glasses of champagne and they fell into a pile of big soft pillows. Our home was a kind of Turkish *fin de siècle* salon with ottomans and palm trees, tiger skins and huge pillows. I'd hide behind a curtain, and in the middle of the action – I would always wait until she was swooning – I would suddenly appear and throw myself between them. Not just once. I did it many times.

'She never knew where I was hiding because I had learned the old ventriloquist's trick of how to throw my voice from just about anywhere. She'd shout, "Where are you?" as soon as she came home with another lover, always a different one. My voice came back from the other end of the house, "Here, Mama!", but where, she could never be sure. Then I suddenly appeared. Her lover would grab me, foaming with anger, and throw me out of the room by the scruff of my neck. Yet I never gave in, not me! I'd cup my hands behind the locked door and shout as loud as possible, "Whore! Kurvah! Putana!"

'If her lover came after me, I'd run away. If she came out herself, I'd spit at her and she'd slap my face until I cried. Then she'd hug and kiss me and cry too, only briefly, and never let me go without a warning: "Next time you spy on me I'll blind you with my very own two hands, so help me God! You shouldn't see your mother naked, you devil! God will punish you for it and if he doesn't I shall!"

'In time I lost my fear and never stopped spying on her, I didn't mind her beatings and threats. I really terrified my poor mother until once she nearly killed me. Still it proves even the Messiah has a mother. He is therefore human. Right? Only too human. Alas!'

Elim turned on his heels, walked along the corridor and took the short staircase up to his floor. I watched him, slightly stooped forward holding on to the rail. An ordinary middle-aged man, a hypnotist, illusionist, professional showman, gifted artist, was walking off stage and back into his private loneliness, after dazzling his audience with a long series of extraordinary tricks. Did he know I was watching him behind his back? He probably did. Of course he did. We all know if, how and when we have left our imprint on people we've just met for the first time. (I still can't decide whether or not he too 'recognized' me as someone strangely familiar.)

I had already packed my suitcases, called the houseboy to take my luggage down to the taxi and was inspecting drawers and cupboards to see whether I'd forgotten something when the phone rang.

It was Elim, of course, giving me a final taste of his psychic powers. 'I know you are off to Berlin.' (How the hell he could know that left me speechless). 'I also know whom you are going to see. Wertheimer. Irving gave you an introduction to him. I know Wertheimer well. You are wasting your time. You'll soon find out. He is richer than I am but he won't give you a penny. He is a fool and a fop. All he thinks of is sex and that kind of nonsense. You'll stay no more than three days, but expect to hear from me.' Then he hung up.

I paid the bill and exchanged flirtatious glances with the cashier who seemed surprised to see me back alive. Well, I am still surprised to be back alive myself.

The flight to Berlin also went via Luxembourg and, to my amazement, I flew back with the same crew and the same forty German ladies and their guide Dr Asmus. We greeted one another like the old friends we had actually become on the way over. I asked everyone about Brother John and Sister Agnes and got the strangest information. I wonder what you make of it. I was told by Captain Strommer himself that the so-called German priest and nun were neither brother and sister nor German. In fact they were Russian KGB agents, a famous couple of spies, and within twelve hours of landing, they had been taken into Icelandic custody and'll remain in jail for some time. Can you believe it? Well, why not?

Here I am in the Kempinsky right on the Kurfürstendamm. After the Icelandic episode when I feared for my life every minute, Berlin feels like a homecoming.

I am curious to meet the infamous Walter Wertheimer, I have heard much about him, and shall write to you in a few days.

Yours, brother Manny

# Letter from Boris Borovsky
# to his brother Emmanuel

The Lodge
Bishop's Avenue
London
15th May

I can't tell how well you are doing with your Redemption
Machine but from the length of your letters I deduce you must
have a first-class electronic portable. Oksana, who also reads
your letters, said yesterday: 'Your brother is as much an inventor as I am prime minister. He likes to move around looking for
the company of exotic characters and seems to have nothing
better to do. Besides, most of what he writes is pure fiction; he
makes it up as he goes along.'

True: Your story from Iceland with your meeting of a Messiah
called Ffinger, who records his own voice into a wooden drum
buried in a sauna in the far north of Iceland, is strong stuff and
I have no idea what you are trying to tell me with this tale. It
all sounds to me like another of your 'inventions'. I try to
psychoanalyse and don't get very far with my diagnosis. Still,
there are two or three clear implications of a dose of mild
depression and schizophrenia.

*One*: you meet yourself in Elim Ffinger and this other self is
very mad, very rich and very paranoiac.

*Two*: you are impressed by his magic as an illusionist; you,
too, would like to be a magician, so you could change your life
at will.

*Three*: you are something of an intellectual homophile; you like to be with women but you don't like discussing anything 'serious' with them. In your heart, like so many fools, you are convinced the female brain is inferior to ours.

On the first two points I raised I have no argument with you. Any form of slight or heavy depression and all kinds of disturbed mental states are normal because they are common. My argument is about the third point.

Women are wiser, much wiser than we are, even the most stupid among them can teach us a few lessons. Every intelligent man knows that – all you have to do is marry one and you'll be convinced.

As far as this is concerned you have to be lucky, of course, but I am cursed. I am doomed to have to share my bed and table with a barren Amazon who is ready to bite off my head. The other night when I came back from a meeting she attacked me like a tigress as soon as I had set foot inside the door. She first screamed obscenities at me. Then she bit and scratched me and practically broke my jaw. I had to slug her before she came to her senses. Then we started to make love as if we were both twenty-two. It practically killed me. All this because I wouldn't let her bring a little rat-like white dog called Nixi into the house.

When everything really gets too much I escape into books. Their function is to subdue our own questionable ideas and make us listen to the firm conviction of another man's voice. Just by listening to the words of others we regain our sanity. All my life I've been faced with the incomprehensible female mystery. 'Faced' is the wrong term; wrapped up in it, like in a shawl, is more correct.

According to Bachofen it's a classical problem, not just my personal one. The trouble started (I quote) 'when men, beholding the beauty of Psyche, neglected the cult and temples of Aphrodite. This pure contemplation of beauty is in itself contrary to the principle represented by Aphrodite. Aphrodite, too, is beautiful and represents beauty, but her beauty is only a means to an end. The end seems to be desire and sexual intoxication; actually it is fertility. Aphrodite is the Great

Mother, the original source of all five elements. When, like the Babylonian Ishtar and the Greek Demeter, she hides herself in anger, the world grows barren. But, after the Lady Ishtar has descended, the bull no longer mounts the cow, the ass no longer bends over the she-ass and the man no longer bends over the woman. The man sleeps in his place and the woman sleeps alone.'

We all ultimately sleep alone and not only in the nether world, but in this one too: that's what it says. But it's not true that Oksana and I sleep separately: we share a bed together. Yet everyone sleeps alone. We won't touch one another, certainly not in bed. When we do touch it's usually in a wrestling match in the hall, on the kitchen floor or under the desk in the library, at times in the corridor or on the upstairs landing.

I embrace you and look forward to your next instalment. To be quite frank: your troubles cheer me up.

Yours, Boris

# Letter from Emmanuel
## to his brother Boris Borovsky

> Hotel Kempinsky
> Kurfürstendamm
> Berlin
> 28th May

Monday

Finding the GRÜNE SPINNE was not easy. Finding Walter at his *Stammtisch*, a walk through Sodom and Gomorrah. As you enter the establishment, past a number of heavyweight boxers dressed in dinner jackets, you are being welcomed by a head waiter, who introduces himself as 'Arnolda', a name as unusual in its feminine form as, for that matter, this weird male/female creature with long black hair, combed to one side, in the fashion of the early thirties. He is something different from what you see in this respect everywhere. Arnolda has moustaches like Dali, wears an open white-ruffled dress shirt over dress trousers and black lacquered shoes. His shirt is only closed on the three lowest buttons, half hiding her/his two large, beautiful firm breasts. That's the reception. I was expected.

He asked me to follow her/him to Walter's *Stammtisch* at the far end of a vast and very noisy bar and restaurant, and walked ahead. A strutting cockerel shaking its feathers on this short walk under an enormous chandelier that was made to look like an enormous light green spider hanging from the ceiling. Reflected in floor-to-ceiling phosphorescent mirrored walls, there were a few interesting sights. I can't describe them all. At one table two middle-aged men were kissing across a cake and candles, clearly celebrating a birthday. At another table further down the aisle to my left, three young girls were licking each other's fingers while making grunting noises. The waiters were dressed half male/half female. Others were made up in such a way that you couldn't tell what was what. The trays on which they carried the food (a mixture of Japanese and French *cuisine nouvelle*), were shaped like fig leaves. Dishes, plates, bowls and silverware made to look like either male or female sex organs. A group of transvestites was involved in a lively discussion on the question of whether or not Raquel Welch is one of their kind. A man of about forty held a hat in front of his open fly, so as not to spill on the ground what is holy to God. It would have equally angered the management. Finally we reached Wertheimer's table.

'You have a visitor, sir,' Arnolda announced in his baritone. The guests and Wertheimer looked up from their glasses. Arnolda pretended to fasten a button on his shirt and touched, as if accidentally, both his nipples. Beaming and smiling faces confirmed this small obscene gesture as a much appreciated little joke in this establishment. Everyone laughed. Cocaine, cognac and champagne made the rounds. Walter is known for his orgies as well as for his spendthrift ways in Berlin – parties that are usually attended by senators, generals, judges, industrialists, and a few 'famous artists'.

He was flanked by two pretty young faces. They looked like identical twins, barely sixteen, and introduced themselves, in high-pitched whispers, as Adrienne and Michelle. Going clockwise, to the right of Michelle sat a beautiful, voluptuous creature of about thirty, all radiant smile and fiery eyes. An orchid in bloom. Pauline Schroeder, the love goddess, who smelled sweetly of roses with musk, a fragrance that goes straight to my groin. She gave me her left hand and said, 'Sorry!' Her right hand was caught between Michelle's thighs. She gave me a big broad, disarming smile. I indicated with the gesture of the upward-turned open palm 'That's OK'. To the left of Pauline sat the 'funny fellow' of the evening.

This *bubikopf* had his hair dyed blond, wore lipstick, powder and rouge and green-painted fingernails. He was dressed in ballet tights, introduced himself as Nicole, 'but you may also call me Klaus, *auf* deutsch'. He told me he was a plumber and bricklayer by profession. '*Maedchen fur Alles, von Berufung.*' The pudgy middle-aged drunk to his left was Werner von Wittelsbach, his boyfriend. First to inspect the labels on the champagne bottles. A waiter made up to look like Marilyn Monroe, except for an overwhelming codpiece in the fashion of fifteenth-century Venetian dandies, placed a chair for me between Werner to my right and Adrienne to my left.

Conversation went on in English and German. Walter's English was perfect. He also has homes in New York, Phoenix (Arizona), Paris and Los Angeles. He said: 'How do you do, *mein Lieber? Setzen Sie sich*, please.'

This was obviously the close circle to try out new ideas for new film projects and celebrate the première of *Der Mann von Buxtehude* – a gothic tale of a noblewoman, Traute vom Amselfeld, who became Cardinal Bishop of Pforzheim in 1542, rode to war against powerful barons with glittering sword, hiding her advanced state of pregnancy behind layers of purple garments. After *Der Mann von Buxtehude* delivers Pforzheim from the Bohemian protestant princes, she gives birth to a healthy pair of twins before the perplexed entourage of marshalls, courtiers and bishops, who raise their crystal beakers to the first true German feminist.

'What next?' Wertheimer asked me. 'Now we have covered the church, feminism, war, treachery and mother love. What's left? *Was meinen Sie?*' I didn't know whether to answer him in jest or seriously, nor did I think it would make much difference here.

'How about a movie,' I fantasized on the spur of the moment, 'about a lesbian motorcycle club called "Heavenly Angels", dressed all in white leather, kidnapping the First Lady on white shining motorbikes? Like Patty Hearst, the victim joins her kidnappers, turns into the fiercest of the Heavenly Angels and swears to take over the Presidency. After a number of hair-raising chases at the head of her motorcycle gang, she fights the President's bodyguards on the lawn of the White House with a silver pistol. All this under the watchful eyes of the world's TV cameras. Tension mounts. The fatal shot is to be fired – the President intervenes in the last second. He refuses to allow his wife to be shot. In a flashback he sees in her his own struggling mother. The First Lady takes over the White House, appoints herself as Commander-in-Chief and Chief of Staff, dismisses all top brass in the Pentagon and orders their secretaries, wives and girlfriends to replace them. Mrs Weinberger, Secretary of Defence, demonstrates before Mrs President a model of the first *female nuclear bomb*. It's shaped like a vagina.

'The First Lady summons the First Dame of the Fleet to her Oval Room (renamed the Ovary Room) to send her to Russia with a plastic model of the new BOMB under glass. Before the fleet sails on its Peace Mission to the women of Leningrad, the First Lady takes the salute at a parade on an aircraft carrier. Suddenly . . . disaster! Sabotage by a male rating in drag of a female officer! A plot by the ousted all-male CIA. The Bomb explodes but instead of showering New York harbour with nuclear fallout, colourful edible tinsel falls like manna from the sky. The shock of the explosion has catapulted the First Lady, her Admiral and ministers, ladies-in-waiting and her body-guards overboard. A handsome sailor among the dozen who jump into the water for rescue brings the First Lady back to shore and back to life by mouth-to-mouth resuscitation. Like the princess in the fairy tale, she wakes up, kisses her rescuer and swoons in his arms, laughs and cries in ecstasy. The President surrounded by his loyal staff arrives in his limousine and smiles when he discovers his wife has obviously regained her senses, in every respect. He leads her away and back to the White House at the head of a ticker tape parade down Fifth Avenue. Call it *Mission Not Accomplished* or something like that and we are in business.'

'That's exactly my kind of movie, *nicht?*' Wertheimer beamed and everyone at his table agreed, of course. I had supposed correctly that I would have to beat them at their own kitsch before I could hope to interest Wertheimer in my prospective invention. That too is quite reasonable strategy. He agreed to meet me tomorrow at the office of his studio in the Grunewald.

Wednesday
Seen from the back, his white hair down to his shoulders, you'd think he was a Shetland pony on its hindlegs. All you see of him from the front is an enormous nose; the rest of his face had been lifted repeatedly to make place for the nose. There is the twinkle of the perennial roué in his small half-closed blue eyes. Another prominent feature are his huge white bushy eyebrows. He dresses in Savile Row suits and his fingernails are manicured. No dirt under his nails. He is muscular and strong like a horse.

When he heard from Irving Cohen that I was an inventor, he expressed interest in an invention to make him live to 184 if not longer, eg another 100 years. It wouldn't surprise me if he did anyway, looking at him. He looks healthier and fitter than most men of sixty. He jogs two miles a day, plays soccer in Berlin, baseball in New York, canoes down the Colorado Rapids in a kayak (says Irving). Only this spring he won the New York marathon for participants over eighty – literally by a nose length. A year ago he started hang-gliding in the Taunus mountains. He also likes free fall parachuting from four thousand feet.

'How does he manage all this?' 'Special diets, special foods.' A Rumanian doctor called Carel Stupescu, physician to the Aga Khan, gives him daily injections of lamb's liver, special lamb's liver, of course, from llama lambs. Two thousand dollars a shot. A Korean company in Alaska breeds for him whales in enormous sea-water tanks fed on ginseng and ground-up deer antlers and tons of plankton. Four thousand dollars for the fluid ounce of ginseng cod-liver oil. His breakfast (I saw it with my very own eyes) consists of half a fertilized ostrich egg, four ounces of Beluga, washed down with two cups of honey mead. 'Keeps me frisky,' he says, while I chew away at my toast and marmalade. He also eats faster than a hungry wolf which I was always told is bad for your digestion.

'Bullshit,' he says, 'nonsense – the opposite is true. I owe my good digestion to fast eating. All that goes in fast, comes out equally fast. Food mustn't be allowed to linger in your stomach linings, that's when it turns to toxic matter.'

'And in spite of this great diet, your doctor told you you are anaemic? Is that true?'

'That's true,' he said, 'I told him not to bother me any longer. I fired him. I can afford to live forever, so why not do it? Financially I can easily survive every crash, every depression, every inflation, every emergency. So far I have survived two world wars, several bouts of inflation and many other disasters.'

People like Wertheimer, who have as much money as he has, feel entitled to an eternal life. He simply wants to live forever. 'And how about the eternal boredom that awaits you? Like God himself, you'd have to watch generation after generation doing the same idiocies. Isn't it like watching a movie with no end and no point? Doesn't the thought alone put you to sleep?'

'Not me,' he said.

'And how about finding suitable lovers?'

He gave me a huge naughty boy's grin. 'My lust for life is too vulgar, too base and simple to go on record.'

'Are women, I mean promiscuity, with AIDS and other plagues going around, not a health risk?'

He waved a hand. 'Women are my professional hazard. Every deep-sea diver soon learns to handle the dangers of the deep or he would never dive more than once. Of course there are sharks and piranha fish – those that may bite off a leg and those that would nibble you to a frizzle. There are poisonous blowfish and slimy, strangulating man-sized eels and water snakes among them, what else? There is all kinds of marine life down in those lower depths where life becomes exciting. I learned to survive them and if you can survive all their female tricks you can survive. Show me a woman I can't handle and

'I'll make her eat out of my hand,' he bragged. 'I don't need a woman's love. All I need is a young body and only that for a while. And a short while will do. I am a very busy man – as you can imagine.'

A slumbering lion, when aroused from his warm middle-aged afternoon nap, remembers he is starving and goes hunting for new prey.

To get him to change the subject, all that was needed was to admire his extraordinary desk, an enormous piece of gothic furniture made of solid German oak, twenty feet long, eight feet wide on solid carved legs. I counted eight of them, each of them telling a different legend of the fruits of the seasons. The cross-bars, six of them, were reliefs in wood, as well as miniature sculptures of maidens with baskets of fruits and flowers pursued by boars, stags and hares, which in turn were chased by half a dozen hunters with bow and arrow, knives and spears. A rustic scene from the German lands made by late fifteenth-century master craftsmen.

Walter came to stand next to me to admire his treasure with the eyes of one who had never seen it before. 'You are looking at the famous Long Table of Teplitz, in the family since 1848. My great-grandfather found it in Dresden in the street. After the uprising. It had been part of a barricade. He only needed a horse and cart to take it home. We have notes on what it looked like when he found it. Part of one crossbar was charred; soldiers had chopped off some of the heads of the geese; one of the foxes had lost its tail and so on. He had it restored by descendants of the craftsmen who built it.

'It's a table of many legends. It once belonged to a Baltic Baroness, one Minerva von Butzhoven, who had bought it from Richard Wagner's wife, Cosima. Wagner supposedly wrote his anti-Semitic pamphlet *The Jews in Music* on this table. When my family left Berlin in 'thirty-nine we stored it with a non-Jewish friend in his villa on the Wannsee. Apparently the Wannsee conference of 1941 took place in our friend's home. He was a professional diplomat stationed in Japan and in his absence the house was requisitioned by the SS. Quite possible that Eichmann, Himmler, Kaltenbrunner, sat around my family's heirloom. A powerful symbol for you to unravel, but then it's also a powerful desk. My enemies planned the destruction of my family on my own family table – and the curse fell back on them. What do you make of that? *Aber man muss vergessen können.*'

Friday

I was wondering after this meeting with Wertheimer whether to go back to the Caymans, where I'm expected. What a total waste of time!

Maybe I am just the old wandering Jew but I can't tell whether it's a curse as long as I am free to move, and what I mean by wasting time I can't tell you either, any more than I can decipher the allegory of Wertheimer's family table. I know that certain German Jews can't change and will first and foremost remain German and feel at home among Germans. There are thirty thousand Jews in Germany.'*Ich bin ein Berliner*, more than President Kennedy ever could be, even though I too have an American passport,' he said.

Well why not? No one forces them to leave so, of course, they don't. Would we have left Poland without being forced to? I might have. You'd probably still be there if it hadn't been for the war. And so would our parents and the rest of our families. And if the communists hadn't destroyed Jewish life and made Jews feel unwelcome after the war . . . If. And what if Hitler hadn't been so insane and had allowed certain Jews to join his Nazi party . . . ? If. All this is mute speculation.

Anyway, my purpose is to discuss my Redemption Machine which could replace the United Nations, the International Monetary Fund and other universal agencies and mete out social justice, providing you press the right buttons.

'What kind of invention?' Wertheimer asked me, and to be funny I said: 'My Messiah runs on 15 watts, uses 110 or 220 volts, and is A/C and D/C.'

62

'Nice idea,' he said, 'but without sex appeal. I have no desire to mess around with computers,' he added, 'unless you can programme one to find me new talent. I am getting bored with the local girls and will reciprocate with a generous cash donation to your pet project if you find me real talent. Beautiful, clever and exciting talent. Be my pimp, in short, and I'll be your friend.'

'It's a deal,' I said, 'and a challenge.'

And you know whom I have in mind? Oksana! Don't you want to get rid of her? She is a natural terrorist. He needs one of those. The man has everything else. Give it a thought, dear brother, this might be your chance. Buy her a ticket to Berlin and you might never see her again. I can feel you don't like this idea either. Masochists and sadists make inseparable marriage partners. I shouldn't forget this little bit of psychology.

Thursday

I swear I had planned to leave tomorrow for New York, where I can stay with friends and compile a list of 'talented' ladies for Walter's consideration. I could do the same in London, but then I might be tempted to stay with you, which is out of the question as long as you are so miserably involved in your domestic drama. I can't see a role for me in this production. . . . Besides, the Messiah called me from Antwerp this morning and asked me to meet him here at the Kempinsky tomorrow for lunch. He mentioned Irving Cohen had rung him the other day, enquired after me and suggested I visit another friend of his who now lives in New York, a wealthy eccentric Georgian from Tiflis who has got it into his head to put a Star of David into orbit!

Friday

What a lunch! I gradually realize who Elim really is. A provocateur. He'd drive anyone into a frenzy with his mad scheme to convert all non-Jews to Judaism by persuading all Jews to become Christians, Muslims, Hindus or Buddhists. 'Redemption must come from within! We are the spark of Divine light in the spiritual darkness of the world, even if we have to become "secular" or "atheist" – if that's the current religious fashion – though it is no longer. It's better to be not Jewish outwardly if you want to be more of a Jew inside.'

The Turk has destroyed his mind. Elim has accepted his calling to be the new Sabbtai Zvi. 'The false Messiah' his enemies called him, when he became a Muslim, while some of his most loyal followers followed his example and still believe in this mad notion of 'the Redeemer in disguise' to this day. I watched Elim eating. He made a five-course dinner vanish within twenty minutes. He eats as fast as his friend Wertheimer, if not faster, so as to have time to take over the conversation. The man can't actually converse. He can only lecture or dictate.

'There is little time left. We must act soon. We must appoint a new UN Secretary, the present one is a petty bureaucrat. We must get Gary Hart into the Oval office – his original name is Herz. We also must replace Gorbachev with Sakharov's wife, Mrs Bonner. I should like to see Miss Bhutto in charge of Pakistan, she is one of us. Her real name is Baruchia, an old Sephardic-Turkish family. One of her ancestors was related to the Messiah from Smyrna.

'Did you know that the present German Chancellor Helmut Kohl had a great-grandfather who still spelled his name with an 'n' and not with an 'l' at the end? He came from Buscacz and was a pedlar. His name was Solomon Ben Mordechai Kohn. I have documents to prove it. I have a library of documents in another hidden place, not in Iceland but in Lichtenstein, in Vaduz, in the vault of the National Bank. Alfonso in Argentine is also a Sephardi, of course, everyone knows that but few people know the real name of the late Mao Tse Tung. Guess.'

'Moshe Zung?'

'You know too much. I need you in my organization.'

'Will you then sponsor my . . . Redemption Machine?'

'Not so fast. But I'll introduce you to a man in Amsterdam

who is a friend. One Bert Alkmaar van Sluys. His father was a martyr. He hid Jews during the war, twelve of them, and was executed by the Gestapo, on the green, right across from the Hotel Americain where you'll be staying. Whether the Dutchman will finance you is also uncertain but he'll listen to you, which is more than I can afford to do. Sorry, I am pressured. I have a meeting in half an hour with von Weizsaecker. He is on a private visit in Berlin – came to meet me. We must solve the Waldheim problem. I have a few ideas in this respect, I wish to discuss them with my friend, Richard. He is also one of us but please keep this information to yourself.'

I promised. He scribbled the name of the Dutchman on a piece of paper, put his reading glasses away and paid the bill. We shook hands and he vanished through the revolving doors into the afternoon traffic. Before I know it, dear Boris, I'll be involved up to my neck in Elim's masterplot to take over the world, but should everything not turn out as expected, Australia Mallone will always be waiting for me with her special treat: chocolate chicken (I hope).

Yours, M.

PS With the sort of people I go around with one can't tell when they are joking and when they are serious. For all I know Elim could well be a personal friend of the President of Germany. What he said about Kohl sounds more unlikely, but I don't have proof this is not so. Does it matter who is and was Jewish? Are the seeds of Hitler's *Rassentheorie* burgeoning again? (Which, incidentally, wasn't his but consisted of ideas mainly borrowed from Austrian, French and British so-called philosophers, who were out to prove the superiority of the white race and foolishly forgot the role of the Jews in European history and the colour of their skin.) Because of all these jokers I mix with, like Irving Cohen and Elim Ffinger, I also forget important facts. I tend to forget there are plenty of racists, white and black, who still hate us either for being Zionists and aggressive, or pacifist liberal fifth columnists or for both . . . like Gore Vidal does. The subject of who is and who is not Jewish and what this 'means' is a timeless topic, eminently suitable to be written and thought about in depth and at great length.

M.

# Letter from Emmanuel Borovsky
## to his brother Boris

Hotel Plaza
New York, N.Y.
6th June

He said I'd recognize him by his white three-piece suit and by his fat square fingers studded with diamonds. He is either in his late or his early sixties. A small grey ring of hair crowns his bald skull. He has the light brown eyes of a hawk, but can be kinder-looking when showing his squint. King of the Ganeffs of Tiflis is his full title. His name is Lew Grusinsky and Irving is convinced he is still KGB. We met in the Oyster Bar for drinks at five and I decided to ask him straight to his face whether he was a Russian agent.

'Me, a Russian agent?' he chuckled. 'Let me tell you a story and you can judge for yourself. Here we go . . .' (I'll tell it the way he did.)

'My father, my grandfather and my great-grandfather were born in Tiflis and that's where I was born. We were manufacturers of ladders even back in the eighteenth century. Then came the Bolshevists in 1917. First they took our factory away but a few years later under Lenin's new economic policy, they gave it back to us. When Stalin came to power, things improved. Now my father could draw a regular salary as a director, which until then he never could afford to pay himself. Then father died in 'forty-eight and Stalin died in 'fifty-three and I was made its new director, and because I am who I am and have not been made with a finger, as we say at home, I soon

67

found out where the money is. Look carefully at a ladder! Study it and you'll see what I mean. The ladder is made of rungs placed at right angles between poles of wood or iron. Correct? Let's say an eight-metre ladder requires sixty-four rungs. You will understand right away that the more rungs you give it, the more expensive such a ladder must become. It's those little platforms that cost the money. What if we use only sixty or fifty-eight rungs instead of sixty-four for our eight-metre ladder? You save rungs, you save money and you can produce more ladders. I introduced the 'people's ladder' – it had less rungs maybe, but it was also thirty per cent cheaper – and for certain customers who wanted to have an old-fashioned capitalist ladder, I supplied them custom-made. And we did very well, thank you. I had seven good years. From 'forty-eight until 'fifty-four. Stalin died in 'fifty-three and Beria was shot in 'fifty-four just one year later.

'With Beria in charge of the GPU, as the KGB was called then, everything went fine and not because *I* needed to work for them. My wife, Tanya, and my daughters, Nadya and Katya, who were then only sixteen and seventeen, bless their hearts, did the work for me. I admit they were beautiful, they still are, but it's a few years ago now. Then they were absolutely stunning. Beria, who loved women even more than he liked shooting kulaks and traitors (as he confessed to me once), was my regular house guest, with one difference. When Beria came to Tiflis, I offered him my hospitality and left. I went sailing and hunting with friends, having a nice males-only holiday. The women were looking after the business. Got my point? At the time I had a friend in Khabarovsk called Igor Godorovosky –' (he spat out). 'May he choke in hell. Godorovsky Igor was a megalomaniac as so many of my friends, true, but this Igor was also mad. *Meshugge.* Just because he had been buying ladders from me for twelve years for his factory where they made gramophone records, and had paid me good prices, he thought he was Beria and that I'd leave him alone with my wife and daughters when he came to Tiflis. Frankly I didn't even like him that much and my women certainly didn't go for him.

'He was handsome in an ordinary way, yes maybe, but he had no class and no culture. Every other word he spoke was "shit" or "fucking". I don't care for such *prolets*. But my ladies were famous even in Khabarovsk for their beauty and grace and Igor wanted to have something to brag about. He could have lied of course. Instead he began to cause me *tsores* – trouble. Long story short: he denounced me to Beria's arch-enemy. Beria behaved like a brother. He warned me and advised me to get out. He issued me with a piece of documentation and even found me an Egyptian who took my savings with him to Cairo in case they wondered at customs how come a Soviet tourist could be in possession of half a million dollars. You see, we always invested in greenbacks. We didn't buy jewels, or dachas or pianos like some of our close friends. This Egyptian Mullah I could trust with any amount of money. You know why? You won't believe it, but such Arabs exist. He told me he had studied our Scriptures and come to the unshakeable conclusion that Allah had promised the land of Israel to the Jews and not to the Arabs! Wouldn't you trust an Arab who believes in the Jewish Bible? I did and didn't regret it. And that's how I came here, not like a pauper but like a rich man, and in this country, thank God, you can make money without having to peddle your daughters and your wife.'

At this moment a statuesque woman in her fifties, who introduced herself as Ludmilla, joined us at the table. 'You'll understand. Tanya left me when we came to New York. Went to Brazil with a Hungarian animal trainer, a *shlemiel*, who works like a fool, and all he has to show for it is a dog or a cat standing on its hind legs and stretching out its paws. He trains them for beggars, who hold their hats out to collect pennies. What a *schnorrer*! My daughters also left me. Not surprising. They are independent. They are not married but they both have rich lovers, which is better and more solid than a dreary marriage. Do you still think I am a KGB agent?'

'I have my doubts,' I told him.

69

'Yes. And now let's go to *tachless*. You'll have noticed that the New Yorkers have taught me Yiddish. At home we only spoke Georgian or Russian. Anyway, I am a great admirer of Israel and I want to do something for my people. What do you think of the following idea: a Mogen David, a Star of David, in the sky, shining down from space with coloured laser beams? Attached to a satellite, it circles the globe and instead of telling people what a superior race we are, we just point up, and there it is! The Star of David like the eyes of God protects the universe, shields all mankind! What else needs to be said?'

'Yes, what do you think?' Ludmilla asked me too, and both looked at me as if I were NASA.

I had to be diplomatic so as not to spoil my chances. 'I think it's a wonderful idea, but maybe even a little more complicated and costlier than my Redemption Machine.'

'And what, if I may ask, is a Redemption Machine?'

'It's the ultimate answer. It doesn't shine with coloured laser beams, it spells out social justice word for word, number for number.'

'What do you think, Ludmilla?' Lew Grusinsky turned to his spouse.

'I think,' she spoke with Solomonic wisdom, 'the gentleman should show us a model or bring us some technical literature. I've never heard of such nonsense! Social justice? What's that? Who needs it?'

'I am afraid Ludmilla is right. Oh, women are so clever! Social justice? What are you, a teenager?'

'It's Jewish philosophy, the essential Jewish mission to the world!' I protested.

'But that's not a symbol of strength. It has no universal application. It's what the poor need and the rich have. First make money, then there is something to share.'

'That's what I came to ask you for. Money. Money to develop my idea.'

He got up and brushed some ashes from his waistcoat. 'It has been a pleasure meeting you, young man.' His wife also shook hands with me and they both left. They even left me to pay the bill.

Now you realize, dear Boris, why this trip to New York was another waste of time, or another experience, depending on how you look at it. Anyway I need to sell you a few more shares in my company. You will then have the majority voting power at our next board meeting, but please send the money by return.

Yours, M.

PS Meanwhile, so as not to be too idle, I'm trying to do some business with Wertheimer as you'll see from the copy attached. For Oksana I'll write him a special newsletter. Agreed?

# From Emmanuel Borovsky
# a message to Walter Wertheimer

Computer printout of available talent compiled
from the international files of Talentscout Inc.
New York June Fourth for personal attention of
Walter Wertheimer of Wertheimer Film G.M.B.H.
Berlin


MARION SASSOON
Aged 32, amateur pianist, speaks Arab, Hebrew,
English and French, good looks of the Sephardic
princess, excellent posture, perfect white teeth,
pleasant personality.
Hobbies: books, music, travelling, dinner
parties, cinema.
Sharp tongue, can be sarcastic and bitchy and
impatient, likes no commitments except regular
sexual activity.


PATRICIA SONDHELM
Aged 34, elegant, tall, blonde, crystal-blue
coloured eyes, a nymph with a sweet enigmatic
smile, lips open and close like flower petals, a
sonorous voice, a strong handshake, woman with a
will of her own.
Hobbies: sunbathing, travelling, cigarette
smoking, drinking, laughing.
Devious, secretive, easily moved to tears,
hypochondriac, good sense of humour, laughs
easily even before joke is finished. Frugal,
careful, calculated but generous, warm-hearted
personality. Highly recommended young widow.


LANA WAXMANN
Aged 31, dark, beautiful, gracious, dark brown

eyes, perfect slender body, heart-shaped lips,
excellent perfume, the fragrance of seduction,
natural partner for the powerful man.
Hobbies: film and video and books, lovemaking,
talking and eating.
Suspicious, frivolous, stubborn, sexually
overheated, exhibitionist but also shy.


## REGINA VAN DOLEN
Aged 37, tall, elegant, dark, straight nose, firm
full comfortable breasts, hips ditto, big strong
white teeth, big generous mouth, dresses like
gypsy queen, striking company, interesting looks.
Hobbies: tennis, hockey, ice-hockey, rowing,
sailing and swimming.
Softhearted, mean-tempered, impatient but also
loving, generous and warm, radiant, optimistic,
moody.


## ZORA FIEDLEROVA
Aged 29, Slovenian actress, militant feminist,
socialist-Trotskyist, anarchist, long red hair,
white Hungarian skin with moles and freckles,
very pretty.
Hobbies: theatre, meetings, demonstrations,
parades, speeches, lovemaking.
Brutal, cynical, offensive, arrogant, sadistic
and sentimental, loyal and sweet.


## NADINE PETROV
Aged 36, handsome Paris-born Bulgarian
aristocrat, tall, blonde and wide-eyed, strong
nose, small mouth, sweet smile, teacher of
Tantra, happy disposition.
Hobbies: love, discussions on esoteric matters,
gossip, fine Indian cuisine, travelling, soft
drugs, no alcohol.
Overactive, overbearing, overloud but also timid,
easily frightened, extremely gullible, kind-
hearted, good dancer.


## NANA SOLDAT
Aged 36, seductive, medium-sized, South African

novelist, cheerful, charming, delightful company, good sport, not jealous, occasionally bisexual. Hobbies: writing and travelling, French cuisine, old wines and new friends, cosy raconteur. Pedantic, long-winded, impatient but also easy-going, relaxed, intimidated, great charmer, faithful friend, wonderful lover with excellent references.

These are just a few on our long list of available talent. Ready to travel at short notice to anywhere on the globe provided full fare and deposit of ten thousand dollars is prepaid to Talentscout Inc. with signature on contract. Please make your special requests known to us in writing and we shall always be pleased to be at your service. Sincerely yours on behalf of the Management of Talentscout Inc.

                                    Emmanuel Borovsky

## Letter from Boris Borovsky
## to his brother Emmanuel Borovsky

The Lodge
Bishop's Avenue
London
12th June

Things have come to a head. I must get rid of her and the sooner the better. I'm deeply disturbed, dearest Manny, or I wouldn't tell you all this. You have your own troubles with the Jewish problem, I have an Eskimo problem at home. Her latest idea is to drive me out of my mind and my home: pictures of dogs all over the house, framed behind glass – even in the toilet a dachshund. Only if you walk on all fours yourself would you have a chance to ignore her mongrel lovers.

And if that's not enough I also need a live, small black monkey! Whether or not I need it, it climbed down my bedpost this morning. I drove it back to the shop it had come from and it nearly cost me my nose and an eye. And that wasn't all. When I came home from the pet shop she was lying in the hall banging her fists and head against the floor. We are beyond argument. I went to my study and mentioned in passing that as the legal proprietor of the tenement I may refuse strangers on my premises at my own discretion. That's the law of the land!

'A picture of a dog is not a dog, and a monkey is not a dog! You liar! You just hate me!'

True, I just hate her. She is the bride of Satan. She could easily, without qualms, castrate me with a razor while I'm asleep. I sniff at all the food and drink she serves me, you can be certain of that.

I am a physical coward now, but I used not to be when I was younger, as you know, and I have a vile temper at times. I just tried to be civil and to warn her what she might expect from me if she carried on like that. She told me to go and have intercourse with mother, the cholera! I should have killed her for those words alone. I was already at my desk, my head filled with Troeltsch, Uhlhorn, and Neumann, my current reading, when she shouted through the closed door: 'Remember, you pigmy! My teeth can still bite steak out of a live bison!'

A little poetic licence but meanwhile, to be on the safe side, I suggest you arrange something with your friend in Berlin. She always wanted to visit Berlin, she told me. For Siberians like her it's the far golden West, remember! She'd take any opportunity to go away alone and have a try at whether or not her magic still works on other men. Of course she is fed up with me too, because I am such an unbelievably stubborn bastard who refuses her the company of a domestic animal! I can't help it. God be my witness: I have tried hard in my mind to reconcile myself to the idea of being married to a dog owner. I can't. I'd much rather eat pork in a Catholic church on Yom Kippur. There are limits to what a man can and cannot tolerate. Offer her to your friend Wertheimer and may she live with him to a ripe old age in peace, amen, the whore.

Remember in your printout to make her attractive, sweet and of kind disposition. You may lie. No, you must lie if we are to get anywhere with our little plan. You may mention that in Greek mythology a woman just like her was the immortal Alcestis. Homer called her 'divine among women' because Alcestis was willing to take death upon herself which had come for her husband Admetus. At eighty-four it's time your friend started thinking. If death should come for him she would make sure he dies in the saddle. She'll screw him to death and he'll go out with a smile. She always tells me she'll mourn for me for seven years if I go and she'll wear black and that this way she'll feel and be more dead than me! Can you follow the logic of the *kurvah?* She is all set to survive me by seven years! I told her not to do me any favours and drop dead before me. That's what it had to come to, dear Manny, I am ashamed to admit. Love drives me insane and gives me gory, vulgar, bloody, monstrous thoughts and fantasies night and day.

Yours, Boris

PS Enclosed please find another cheque for two thousand pounds. Enjoy it! Have a good time with redeeming the world but meanwhile don't forget your embattled brother about to be strangled by the demon Lilith.

# Letter from Emmanuel Borovsky
## to Boris Borovsky

Hotel Americain
Leidsekade
Amsterdam
22nd June

Thanks for the cheque which reached me two days ago via New York. Holland looks better for it, if you have a few pennies to afford the patience it needs to get something done here. You'll find me usually on the terrace in front of the hotel, in the Churchill Room or in the lobby when it rains, and it rains, and it has been raining most of the time since I arrived.

Or I stand at my window overlooking a piece of the Leidse-kade canal with a few moored pleasure-boats. I can also look straight into the crowns of three elm trees which half hide the brick wall of the Hotel Merriot across the square on the other side of the bridge. Streetcars clatter past, followed by hordes of cyclists. A street organ grinds out old waltzes. One might imagine the whole world to be at peace, just like this calm, ordinary sober town around lunchtime on a summer's day.

Yesterday Bert Alkmaar van Sluys and I met finally downstairs in the coffee house, an architectural relic from the twenties. Alkmaar is about fifty-five, slim build, clear-eyed and tight-lipped. Ffinger was right, he can listen for hours. I spent three-quarters of an hour telling him how I, moved by the general idea of abolishing hunger and illness in the so-called Third World, had begun to wonder whether a non-political, non-opinionated pragmatic device would not know how to cope more efficiently than human agencies with the scandals of half the world starving while the other half drowns in unspeakable plenty. We can't leave the solutions of what to do with this misery to pure human emotional decision-making. Computers, especially super computers as I foresee them, are the best level-headed authority to implement new economic programmes. As a level-headed Dutchman he'd understand the idea behind my mechanically-minded solutions to a heart-aching universal moral problem.

He let me talk like this for a while but finally opened his mouth. 'We have plenty of morals and morality in this part of the world but, despite all our ethical education, we had our troubles during the war with your people. "Be your brother's keeper," the old book says, but where to keep them all? One man's head saved could mean another man's head lost. My father, as you know, of course, was a war hero, a martyr. He was shot just here across the bridge on the green. Public execution was a warning that the Nazis meant business. We had thousands of traitors in the country who sold their own kin to the Gestapo for reward, out of conviction or simply out of fear. Of course we let the *moffen*, the Germans, take away our Jews. We had no choice. It hurts to think what a lousy lot a Christian nation is. We'll always feel indebted to the Jews, for letting us do it to them and for still coming back here and praising us to boot.'

'It's all relative,' I began my apology but he wouldn't have any of it.

'No, we Dutchmen stink, just like the rest of Christianity and given a choice I'd much rather be a Jew. But that's impossible. I'm too old to get circumcised and just by calling myself a Jew I can't fool anyone, least of all myself. If you could bring me a detailed budget, I might be able to do something for you. I could always write it off on my tax-return as an investment gone bad. But I need a budget, I need to see numbers, so I know what we are talking about.'

'We are talking about ending hunger and sickness and infant

mortality among the underprivileged tribes of Africa and Asia. We are talking about ethical principles.'

'Not without a budget sheet. We agree on the principle. Now we have to discuss the cost of salvation, that's obvious.'

It had never been made so obvious to me until I met an ethical Protestant Dutchman that the price for the redemption of mankind cannot be paid by men of good will who have the souls of accountants. In the end I'll need government grants. I am getting tired of my mission. I could need a rest, but a rest is out of the question for the time being. Elim Ffinger arrives tomorrow in Amsterdam. He'll just have time for a cup of coffee he told me on the phone. He's meeting with the Chief Justice of the World Court in the Hague. I have no idea why but I shall ask him tomorrow.

Thursday

Ffinger has offered me a position as his correspondent and courier. He suggested four hundred pounds a month for travel costs and six hundred as a starting salary. Of course I accepted and forgot to ask him why he has to go to the Hague.

'Correspondent? What does it mean?'

'I'll be more specific. I want you to go to Vienna tomorrow and look up a man called Hofrat Professor Doktor Franz U. Heimlich. He was a big Nazi during the war and rumour has it that he has genuinely repented and is looking for Jewish recipients of private restitution payment for which ex-Nazis have donated large sums. These are to be shared out among deserving and struggling geniuses like yourself. Were either of your parents by chance born in the former Austrian crown-land of Galicia?'

'Both my parents. Cracow and Czernovitz.'

'Good enough. Then you qualify as a former Austrian.'

'But I am British!'

'Only on your passport! You'll always remain a Galician.'

'I was born in Congress Poland, not in Galicia.'

'Never mind. Your parents were Galicians and we are the

product of our heritage. Place of birth and passport are incidental information. Write to me about your Vienna encounter with Heimlich.'

He scribbled the following name on a piece of paper: 'Otto, Rudi's Zigeuner Bar, Singerstrasse.'

He got up to leave. 'Incidentally I have done some research: Kreisky is not a Jew. He doesn't know it yet, but I have proof. The Kreiskys were called Kreuzmeier and are Sudetan Germans who married into a half-Spanish, half-Hungarian family called Weiss, back in 1762 in Pressburg. The name Weiss sounds Jewish and usually is, except in this particular case, Zsoltan Weiss was actually Zsoltan Horvath, a Hungarian artistocrat who was in business with Jews. No, Kreisky is a goy. I have proof and I intend to make it public. You'll be surprised what this will do to the Waldheim supporters. The socialists should have made Kreisky their candidate for President of Austria but they were nervous of presenting to the world a Jewish ex-Chancellor for president and a controversial figure at that. Had they known that he is one of them and not one of us, they would have won the elections. Please keep this secret under your hat until you read about it in the *New York Times*.'

I promised. He handed me a fat cheque. Things are moving in the right direction!

I have become privy to quite a few sensational top secrets recently but see no reason why I should not share them with you, my poor brother.

I can't tell you how much I empathize with your ordeal. But: 'Love is stronger than death,' it says in the *Song of Songs*. You cannot be helped. You are lost and doomed and no one can do anything for you. Write to me in Vienna, at the Hotel Imperial (I can now afford it on my new salary). A rich employer at last! That's what I always wanted. I might have found him. Keep your fingers crossed.

PS Attached is a telex message I dispatched to Berlin only yesterday.

84

OKSANA LIEBLICH
Aged 38, a unique and very special personality,
blonde, fiery and outspoken, attractive,
forceful, docile, sweet and of a kind
disposition.
Hobbies: hunting, shooting, fishing, bridge and
rummy, domestic animals, children.
Supreme lover and flirtatious companion, nervous,
quick, bad-tempered, extremely loyal, devoted,
gracious, pleasant speaking voice. Also good
singer, amateur opera buff, delicious-smelling
ripe peach of natural healthy complexion.
Something very special and available only by
personal invitation via the undersigned.

Emmanuel Borovsky


A few things I just made up to make her sound more attractive. The one thing I forgot to mention was the Greek mytholo-
gical bit. Let him find out for himself what a treasure she is.

I'll call you as soon as I hear from Berlin. Meanwhile you'd
better prepare her gradually for this Berlin trip and, for God's
sake, don't change your mind at the last minute. Pull yourself
together. Remember the good days, when you were a bachelor
in between marriages? Those times were not too bad. You were
a free man who could come and go and do as he pleases. Keep in
mind: man wasn't born to be a slave, least of all a slave to his
passions. Be a free man again, Boris! I wish you luck and
embrace you.

Yours, Manny (your
little brother who still
looks up to you with
respect and love)

## Letter from Emmanuel Borovsky
## to his brother Boris

Hotel Imperial
Kaerntner Ring
Vienna
27th June

Why does everything Ffinger plans and does have to be the way
things are in a spy thriller? I suppose he likes it that way. Why
not give me straight the name and address of the ex-Nazi and
his private restitution fund organization, which is so secret only
my Viennese friend Armin knows about it? Through Armin I
also met Elim. Armin is well informed. The organization is
constituted like a Masonic Lodge and called BLUE DANUBE
(he told me). Officially it's a travel agency and sells tickets to
the Salzburger Festwochen, the Spanish Riding school at the
Hofburg, and this kind of attraction.

Anyway I found Otto in Rudi's Zigeuner Bar in the Singerstrasse. Looked as if he had been sitting there in the same
corner for the past three years. A lonely melancholic drinker,
the sporting, mountaineering, alpine type – a ski instructor who
has hit the bottle, dressed like a wedding guest. When I mentioned my name Otto first looked baffled, but after thirty
seconds something must have clicked and he said: 'Hraczek,
Kaerntnerstrasse.' It was just around the corner. Hraczek is a
well-known furrier that sells overpriced sables and minks.
When I whispered my code word 'Otto', a small woman of
undefinable age and looks told me to wait a moment.

The woman stepped behind a mirror and out stepped an

appetizing creature with long blonde flowing hair dressed in white mink. Sheer magic! She was not wearing much underneath except for a suspender belt and stockings, I noticed. I repeated the word 'Otto' and she wrote 'Stubenring 19' on a scrap of paper and gave it to me. She looked at her small diamond-studded watch. 'Franzi is at his office and expects you now.'

Number nineteen is the former Palais of the Polish Duke of Czernovsky, a post-war conversion into a luxury office building, situated right across the entrance to the Stadtpark, the municipal gardens, whence came the smells of flowers and freshly mown lawns. The vast gates to number nineteen are of carved oak, leading to a wide passage and an inner courtyard. A huge glass door to the right of the porter's lodge leads to the lift, up a few marble steps to the left, flanked by a pair of white alabaster lions, at rest, with their paws stretched in front of them, but observing and watching.

Inside the stairwell the place smells of brass polish and cleaning fluids, especially of turpentine and spirit of saltpetre. I rang the bell on the fifth floor beside a brass plaque which read *Blaue Donau G.m.b.H.* The woman who opened it could well have been a twin of the woman in the fur shop who had vanished within seconds (and had either turned into the tall attractive blonde or genuinely disappeared) and here she was back again. Yet it wasn't the same woman. This one had reddish dyed hair, the other one's had been dark brown or even black.

She showed me where to hang up my umbrella and coat, though I carried neither, and led me into a small elegant waiting room. She said she'd tell the 'Chef' I was there. She didn't get very far. The CHEF must have heard me, came out, grabbed my hand and pulled me into his office. A salon with high ceilings framed by mouldings with flower patterns. Huge wide windows with double glazing gave a view over the park but were closed to keep out the noise of traffic from the boulevard and martial music from the lunchtime concert on the bandstand in the park. Red velvet curtains were fastened to the sides of the windows to accentuate the feeling of a proscenium, a classic Viennese interior. A desk fit for an admiral stood beside the window, behind it an armchair from which one imagines the Emperor Franz Joseph might have ruled his Habsburg Dynasty.

A large tapestry depicting the Battle either of Austerlitz or Koenigsgraetz covered one wall. The wall opposite the windows consisted of two glossy white connecting doors leading to the adjoining salon. An ancient Persian rug covered the centre of the polished parquet floor. A sofa upholstered in red, with carved mahogany legs, a green velour Biedermeyer chair, a coffee table of white marble. That was all. The salon felt vast, eerie and empty.

Heimlich, tall with grey hair cut short, studied me out of his watery blue eyes which contrasted with the dark red of the sofa. While talking in an even, monotonous voice he gesticulated wildly – with a hand turned up, hands clasping, a pointed finger, a thumb moved rapidly. The funds available for racially persecuted Austrians or their heirs, he explained, were given with no strings attached, though it's understood, of course, that anyone who signs the receipt for a certain sum has by the same token endorsed an appeal to the world at large to let bygones be bygones. It all makes sense, no? Restitution, financial compensation for past injustices suffered is the one and only logical solution for everyone to find a way back into a world of form and order. The words 'hope', 'youth', 'future', 'world peace', 'tolerance', 'forgiveness' and 'mutual understanding' danced from his lips like elves on Midsummer Night. His manner, his Austrian lilt, his smiles, were as seductive as his analysis of endemic Austrian anti-Semitism which, he claimed, is a result of a specific Austrian weather condition called the *Foehn*, a warm wind that blows from the south over the Alps and makes people go barmy.

'It's the *Foehn* that does it to our rednecks and fatheads. But, thank God, the post-war Viennese air has dramatically improved and in the end all's well that ends well. It ended, thank God, with the defeat of the German war machine and the *Führer's* suicide! It's all simple enough,' and (as he noticed I was reluctant to sign away my last bit of resentment) he added: 'I know the simple things are not always so simple. I suggest you think about it and when you have given it enough thought you come back and you'll always be welcome. We have accounts to settle with you people, overdue, outstanding settlements to make.'

I don't know what kind of inventor of Redemption Machines I will make if I lack the guts to put my signature to such lofty intentions as peace, hope and the future. Yet I'm not, I am still not ready to shake an outstretched hand for the sake of my private folly.


On board Swissair
Flight 506
Vienna – Zürich


By the time I had left his office it was five and, though I tried to make a direct El Al flight to Tel Aviv, leaving at seven, I missed the plane and have taken the next flight out. It happens to be a Swissair going to Zürich and Geneva. Zürich has been on my mind for some time. Zürich is Max Kalischer, the heart specialist and cabbalist. I need my head and heart examined. I have been treading water on Quixotic mills for some time now and maybe for far too long and need sound consultation. I have no appointment with Kalischer but won't leave the Hotel Bel Lac until I see him. Bel Lac, Zürich – that's where you should write to me. Keep your chin up!

Yours, M.

## Letter from Boris Borovsky
## to his brother Emmanuel

Chelmsford
Essex
30th June

Dear Manny,
Your two letters reached me. I would have answered you
before, but I didn't know how to begin to tell you what has
happened. How can I tell you what's on my mind? What
ever has happened to my pride and self-esteem, to my dignity, my courage? What has so changed my heart, defiled my
honour, destroyed my reason, that I would stoop so low as to
kill a dog?
   'A dog and not a man, you coward? Shame on you.'
   Had Josh Brown been a man, I might have gone to jail for the
rest of my life. Fortunately Josh Brown was a three-month-old
cocker spaniel with large, dark, soulful eyes. The fact that we
judge human crimes by human standards plus the fact that I
could prove I had fulfilled his only wish – all these facts together
got me into the Herzweg. When they came for me and said:
'Pack your things, you are going away for a few weeks,' I did as
I was told and stepped into the ambulance. When they took my
things away at the reception, I did not complain. I honestly
didn't care where I was going to sleep. In a noisy ward, a cold
and lonely cell or with Oksana in a warm cosy bed. I felt no
remorse, no need to deny anything. I have the evidence in
writing, if proof is needed. Our correspondence makes that
clear. His last letter is dated 4th June.

Dear Mister Borovsky

The author of this is a poor canine. On this terrestrial plane he cannot compete with you. Maybe he can and will in the next world, where our souls, human and animal, shall meet once more. In our vale of tears my four feet are my handicap. Can a poor four-footed creature blame God for not having created it with two hands? Alas, He didn't make us with hands and that's why I can neither strangle you nor shoot you dead, or I would have done so long ago in cold blood. Take my word for it. God didn't give us hands but He gave us noses bigger than yours. And I can read your mind with my nose. I clearly read that you want to throw me out, send me away. Don't. Kill me instead and the sooner the better. I'd rather be dead than separated from the woman I love.

I cannot live without her and Oksana cannot cope with both of us. She may be your wife but she is my woman, a frail, ordinary woman, at that. And I love her. And she is all mine. When we are alone and you are not around to listen, she confides how much she is in love with me. She really loves me, my bitch. She tells me everything. She tells me she thinks only of me when she embraces you; when she seems to melt in your arms and shows you the whites of her eyes, her pupils are focused on me. Even when she looks at you, I know she sees only me and when you kiss her, it's my tongue she feels. She tells me why she has to lie to you and must go on lying to you: because you will never understand that a love not consummated is a love eternal and, though you may never believe it, our love is stronger than even death itself. That's why I beg you: Please, please kill me. Please. Yours, Josh Brown.

I waited two days before I answered him. I didn't want his blood on my hands. But the words, 'Please, please kill me' dance before my eyes. I lose my reason, my composure, my sleep, my appetite. I go slightly insane. I shop for a gun and find one the very same day. Back home I wait. I am a coward. I am waiting for him to look the other way.

Yet, I want to give him a last chance. I write back.

It's your life or mine. You have a choice. Get out. Scram! Go to hell! Get lost! Find yourself another mistress. This is your last warning. I do have two hands, thank God. I can handle a gun and I will. You seduced Oksana but you won't hoodwink me. You may exploit the feeble sentiments of a poor childless woman but not mine. I'll wait two more days. But if you haven't left by Thursday morning you'll be a dead dog. And good riddance to you. I am not your friend.

I wait two days. He doesn't move. He looks at me from the other end of the room. He peeks at me from behind flowery curtains. He is afraid of me and rightly so. I hold back until Oksana leaves the house to do some errands. I fire. Right between his ears.

When she comes home and sees what has happened, she says: 'You'd better go to the Herzweg for a while.' I have no voice to answer her with. I'm like putty, like wax in her hands. I am her bedbug. She holds me between thumb and forefinger and when she squeezes I expire. But I still have hope. Now you know where you can find me. At the Herzweg Clinic. Come and visit me!

Yours, Boris

# Letter from Emmanuel Borovsky
## to his brother Boris

Hotel Bel Lac
Limmatquai
Zürich
6th July

First things first: are you certain it's called the Herzweg, the place you are in or is it still the Old King's Hall in Chelmsford? The reason I ask you that? Twenty or more years ago I knew a man called Viktor (or was it Bernard?) Kohnstamm who had opened an annexe to his clinic in Jerusalem. I believe you met him as well. A tall, strong, cheerful-looking Viennese, a delightful character, a little pompous and pedantic, as Viennese professors tend to be, but a great charmer.

Remember I had this psychiatrist friend Lorni Rank who went mad one day and tried to stab his father? I used to visit him at the Old King's Hall and as I went quite frequently (once we two drove together, you must recall this!) I became friendly with Kohnstamm, even after they released Lorni and let him go back to Edinburgh where he became England and Scotland's most sought-after shrink in the fashionable cult of the sixties, which produced Oscar Ichazo, John Lilly, Alan Watts, Fritz Pearl, Arthur Janov. An entire generation of priest/psychologists who knew how to rob people of their last privilege (which is staying innocently confused in their own personal way instead of adapting themselves to the whimsicalities of their gurus).

Anyway if the same Kohnstamm is still in charge at the Old

King's Hall I know where to pull a few strings. A good lawyer and the signature of two psychiatrists would also help. All they have to certify is the truth: provoked by your wife's exotic antics and foul language you acted in self-defence! The dog might well have been trained to attack you and tear you to shreds! You couldn't know that, could you, now! You had to kill to save your life – but if you don't like this line, throw yourself on the mercy of the courts and plead that you acted out of wounded pride, in a fit of jealousy. Whichever way you approach the question, there is no way they can lock you up for long. Meanwhile enjoy your stay as a holiday away from home.

After saying all this I hope you realize how lucky you are, dear brother (I still get so angry, I could kick your backside when I think of it!). You could also have shot Oksana by mistake and be inside for at least ten years before they'd allow you out on parole, or you could have, God forbid, shot yourself and be lying six feet underground in a place you'd never get out from, not even if my Messiah Elim Ffinger came to take over the ruling of the world. (I retract my words: if and when they get around to installing Elim as the Messiah anything is possible, I admit. After all one of the Messiah's most important missions is to resurrect the dead.) So in a way it's better for me not to see you right away, because I am angry, I am pissed off with my big brother, who aims a gun at a dog and can't think of a better target. I can think of quite a few better targets, but that's another story. Or is it?

I wish I could forget, erase from my mind, my visit to Vienna. 'Sign here and collect,' he said with a smile. I had the eerie feeling of witnessing a meta-physical, meta-historical meeting between Jacob and Esau (but in strangely reversed roles), when Jacob conned Esau into signing away his birth-right, the blessings bestowed on the first-born, for a dish of lentils.

Think of it. The pre-war Nazi theoretically usurps the ideas of racial purity from the Jews and immediately and 'logically' turns the idea into a legal licence for murder, and persecution.

The wartime Nazi converts a misunderstood idea into the gruesome mass slaughter of millions of totally innocent people. And the post-war Nazi wants to pay for his own stupid interpretation of a natural and all-too-human instinct (reshaping clannish and tribal special interests into a national consensus) and his subsequent idiotic blood orgy on our nation, with the wounded party's forgiveness! It doesn't mean we should refuse restitution necessarily when it's offered to needy survivors. It means there is nothing to restitute where there is no need to do so.

And, speaking of my own objective, maybe my research on computerized universal social justice can wait a little longer. After the old generation of Nazis has died out, forgiveness is useless anyway, as it cannot be passed on to the next generation. Where there is no crime there is no need to be either punished or forgiven. Every bullet fired at a dog is a bullet wasted on your real enemy, and we know their names, names which sound much more *unheimlich* than Franz U. Heimlich. But enough of that.

I am sitting in the Kronenhalle, Zürich's best restaurant, and waiting for a call from Kalischer's secretary to say when it will suit the old man to see me. That's why I have plenty of time for meditation. Above the seats on the right wall of the establishment hang the pictures of famous literati and politicians who filled their stomachs here and got drunk on the excellent local wines.

Above me I can see the twisted smile of the great Dubliner James Joyce, who preferred his exile among the Calvinist Swiss to his home among his outrageous Catholic countrymen, for all sorts of reasons. Above the entrance to the kitchens across my seat, nineteenth-century mosaics of Zürich's craftsmen. Bakers, butchers, masons, carpenters, shoemakers, tailors and tinkers. Each one of them also gets a lofty rhyme in golden gothic letters for his toils and troubles. What I like about this place is the starched table linen, the heavy silver cutlery and the solid legs of the aged waitresses thrust into high laced boots from which tips and heel have been cut away. And what wonderful food! Rich soups and fresh meats and vegetables and crispy baked potatoes! It all tastes like the oranges of paradise, like a Friday evening meal at home.

Waiting for the phone call, which never came, I had a six-course dinner. It took me over two hours, and still no news. Solomon calls Kalischer 'the man of the Hebrew letter *vav*'. Kalischer recently published a paper at Tuebingen University in which he proves how one single letter, the *vav*, which means *and*, turns both past and future into present. If you read the Scriptures with this new interpretation you know God never spoke, nor will speak, but speaks now and always in the present tense. A cabbalist genius and heart specialist all in one.

Saturday
Went to see the great man yesterday and would have gladly spent the rest of my life in his company. He has the presence of a teacher who speaks wisdom with every syllable he utters. The check-up was soon over. My heart is OK though he recommends me to take it (meaning life) *maessig und regelmaessig*: 'Smoke and drink but in moderation and lead a more regular life.' That's not what I wanted to hear.

He also advises more physical activity, including sexual; for which I never find time. I thought my despair (I might be useless and so is everything I do) was the cause of my anxiety attacks. He attributes them to my need for an imminent threat to my life, without which I cannot function. He thinks I'm collecting stories under the pretext of enlisting financial support for a machine which (should it ever have to be built) will certainly be constructed one day by professionals who are constantly building super computers of all kinds. So as not to feel I am wasting my time I should consider writing it all down. If this is done fairly amusingly and intelligently it might be a more useful creation than a 'Redemption Machine' which solves all the world's problems at the pressing of a few keys. Anyway, the technologies are similar to writing, he says. The

98

question he raises is: whether the world's problems really need solving that urgently. More or less like you, he believes that the world only appears to be imperfect to our eyes so that we should try to perfect it. While trying, we exist. And that's all there is to it! I too am no longer convinced that my project is all that urgent. There are always three possibilities:

*One*: I may go back to Australia Mallone on Alligator Island. *Two*: I may go back to Paris and start living with Michèle Portois, for the third and last time; and *three*, there is still the final possibility. If they have changed the management again at the George Cinq I may be able to persuade a new man of the importance of my very presence in his hotel. It took me no time at all to convince Charles de Tour that I was his best insurance policy against terrorist attacks. (How? I simply sent myself coded messages signed with obscure names and showed myself in the company of louche characters.) To be friends with the underworld of gangsters and terrorists made me a welcome guest at the hotel and now that I am in the employ of an Agent of the Divine Almighty, well, I would have something to brag about, I could drop names like small change, the way Elim Ffinger and Irving Cohen do.

I am leaving for Jerusalem tomorrow to see Etan Horowitz. More about it in my next letter. I shall be staying at the King David. You must have plenty of time to collect your thoughts and write me a note.

Yours, M.

# Letter from Boris Borovsky
# to his brother Emmanuel Borovsky
# in Jerusalem

Old King's Hall
Chelmsford
Essex
12th July

At her last visit Oksana read me your letter. I don't know what
has happened to my reading glasses, since I got here. I can't
find anything. I might have left them at home. Oksana says she
can't see them anywhere. Perhaps I have just lost them, but I
can't get new ones. It's not all that easy to persuade an opthal-
mologist to come here. No one believes that a patient will read
or ought to read.

What do I do all day? I walk around the grounds and
wonder. l wonder about everything. How God makes the world
and what he will do after he is tired with it. I don't think God
*made* the world. I agree with your Professor in Zürich, everything takes place only *now* and neither *before* nor *after*. I also
wonder what I would have done differently if I had been God.
The thought keeps me awake at night.

My other concern is: water. How much water does the world
need? It never stops raining in this godawful place. In London
it rains but also stops. Here it only rains. Every day, every
single day and all day long and even at night. It rains and rains
and the skies still remain dark and grey. I never leave my room
unless I want to get wet. I just sit here at the window and look at
the lawn and the trees and the river in the distance and think of
where I would have been at this moment had I not lost my

temper over a stupid dog. I know I'll eventually get out of here, but by the time they let me go I wonder whether I will still care enough to leave.

Yours, Boris

# Letter from Emmanuel Borovsky
## to his brother Boris

Hotel King David
Jerusalem
19th July

Dear Borshu,

Something must be going badly awry with my memory. I remember in my last letter I said: I know a Kohnstamm in England who was in charge of a mental home in Jerusalem called the Alexander Herzweg Clinic, but had opened a clinic near London where I once visited a friend and wasn't sure what it is called. The place you are in must be the Old King's Hall because the Alexander Herzweg is still in Jerusalem, where it always was, and doing better than ever. By sheer coincidence I arrived the day an International Conference of Psychiatrists was opening in the very same beautiful old building. A timeless Victorian mansion, built from Jerusalem rock right in the heart of Jerusalem's German Colony, the old Templar Colony.

The building itself dates from 1865 and is surrounded by a wonderful big garden, a little neglected now the Arab gardener is getting on in years, but still an island of peace and tranquillity in this noisy city.

It happens every time I come here and it happens to other people too, not just me. All kinds of things coincide in mysterious ways. It soon turned out the man we knew in England is not the same Kohnstamm who runs the Alexander Herzweg in Jerusalem. The Kohnstamm we met in England is a nephew of this one. His name is Bernard Kohnstamm. The man here is his uncle, Viktor Kohnstamm. Yet both clinics are more or less one and the same, like two branches of the same banking house. Both run by a Kohnstamm, uncle and nephew. For a while, a short while only, the nephew renamed the Old King's Hall, Alexander Herzweg, but later reverted to the old name. Anyway in case you don't know by now, you are in the Old King's Hall! The confusion arose because Bernard K. told me at the time his uncle had been a refugee in England and left for Palestine in 1940, during the Blitz, bygone days none of us will ever forget.

As I wrote to you from Vienna: I came here to see an industrialist and financier called Etan Horowitz. I had met him many, many years ago in Paris at a dinner party and was spellbound by his adventures as the second-in-command of Israel's Intelligence back in the War of Independence of 1948. In particular his amusing story of how he hired two German hustlers to spy on Egyptian officers in a Cairo nightclub left a lasting impression on me. Etan is a wealthy patriot, you can still meet a few of his generation. ('Better one rich patriot than two *schnorrers* for a friend,' father used to say.) I finally got him on the phone (he was cruising at 70 m.p.h. on the way to the Dead Sea for a swim). He is under such pressure the only available time left to meet is during the 'conference', the most exciting event in Jerusalem since Sadat's visit.

'What is it all about?'

'Ever heard of a Messiah from Antwerp called Elim Ffinger?'

'Not for more than six weeks,' I said. Meanwhile I have also found out that Viktor Kohnstamm knows Etan, who, like all Israelis, knows everybody. I'll have the unexpected, surprisingly unexpected, opportunity to discuss your case. . . . I shall soon report more to you. I want to get this one off in the post instantly, so that you know I am thinking of you a lot and always affectionately.

Yours, M.

## Letter from Oksana Borovsky
## to her brother-in-law Emmanuel
## Borovsky

The Lodge
Bishop's Avenue
London
23rd July

Dear Brother-in-law,
I am the wife of your brother Boris. I have read your letter.
The bastard deserves all he gets. I visit him twice a week. He
showed me your letter. I also read all your other letters. Sometimes he asked me to read them out loud. I don't know what he
writes to you, but I can imagine. I don't even want to know. I
am glad he is safe at the Old King's Hall (you are right, the
Herzweg is called Old King's Hall). The director is pouff. The
nurses is shit. The doctors is quacks. The food stinks. The
service is disgusting. The medical care negligible. The house
smells of . . . cat piss. But my Boris deserves every bit he gets.
Violent, aggressive bastard and murderer he is.
   Now something else. I went to Berlin. Yes I went to Berlin
and I met your friend Wertheimer and I like him. I think he is a
wonderful man. More wisdom in one toe than my Boris in his
big head. More charm, more flair with women, more wit and
much more money than my Boris. Tell you the truth, I fell in
love with the man, and now I tell you a secret: I think he fell in
love with me too. I stayed with him a whole week. He carried
me in his arms, as if I were an invalid, imagine! He is strong like
my uncles on my mother's side. He picks up a woman, a woman
like me, and carries her in his arms!! Whenever I asked my

Boris to pick up a match from the floor he tells me he has a hernia. Dear brother of my husband! Don't worry about Boris. He is happy and he gets what he deserves. I won't leave him there forever. Don't alarm yourself. When I get married to Walter (who sends me forty-eight roses every week through Interflora) I'll put in a good word for poor Boris and they'll let him out. And then what's he going to do? I and my new husband will be travelling to see the world and my poor Boris will sit alone in our big house and wish to God he had a dog, a cat, a mouse, anything to keep him company. Your brother is a melancholic and he is very dangerous.

I don't do him a favour to help him to get out now. He'll be lost and helpless, go out and buy another gun and this time shoot himself through the head. He should have done it, the devil he is, instead of murdering a small puppy. When I think of Josh my heart aches. When I read his last letter to Boris – what a beautiful letter! – I cried and cried all night long. A provisional wedding date has been fixed. We'll get married in New York on October 15th and you are invited. We shall marry in the Temple Beth Emmanuel on Fifth Avenue. Six hundred invited guests. Reception to follow at the Waldorf Astoria! Probably the best thing ever happened to me is to find a gentleman of eighty-four for a lady of only thirty-eight.

Your sister, Oksana

# Message from Walter Wertheimer
# to Emmanuel Borovsky

Harzallee 2
Grunewald
Berlin
22nd July

Thanks, my friend. I met Oksana the evening she arrived and took her to Rumpelmayer. The German language made her so nervous and itchy, she tried to speak her own kind of German, speaks it like I speak Spanish. She said to the waiter: *'Sie machen in mein Kaffee?'* In German it means you suspect someone has pissed in your coffee. 'Go and make a coffee' is what she wanted to say, the way they talk in her igloo up in the Arctic Circle to a younger brother. To my chauffeur she said: *'Sie farten wie eine Windhund.'* *Fahren* and *Farten* is the same to her ears. She amuses me. In bed she was like a tractor on a collective farm, ploughed me over until I fell apart. Had to knock her out with a litre of port before she stopped. She left me exhausted, asleep. When I woke up I noticed a small card tied to my penis. 'Love from your focking Highness.' (I once called her princess and since then she always wanted me to address her as 'Your Highness'.) She advised Charles my butler (who is seventy) to have an affair with a sweet poor girl of fourteen who visits her uncle Fritz, my driver: she told Charles he should do the same as his employer. As I, his employer, seduce young girls, he has every right to do the same. 'Grab her and fock her on the back seat of his Rolls Royce!'

I finally got rid of her, it took me a week. I'm sending her flowers, promise her anything, even marriage, as long as I can keep her away from me. Thanks, friend, for trying to find me something different. She is indeed an incomparable nightmare! No not this one, thank you. Let's discuss your 'Unaccomplished Mission' instead. I liked your scenario very much. Why don't you put it on paper and let us talk about it?

Yours, Walter
Wertheimer

PS As to the other ladies you mentioned in your computer printout, now I have tried your 'speciality', all I can say is the others could only be much worse. Still, if they happen to come to Berlin – you may give them my number.

W.W.

# Letter from Emmanuel
## to his brother Boris Borovsky

Hotel King David
Jerusalem
28th July

What a day! At 9.30 am the lobby was packed and so was the vast conference hall. It was 'by invitation only' – and hundreds of grumbling people were turned away. Etan briefed me with another bit of exciting news. The Messiah from Antwerp – my Samuel Butterfeld alias Elim Ffinger – also happens to be the clinic's sole benefactor and its major shareholder. It's a unique case when a patient who owns the clinic he is in needs the support of eminent psychiatrists around the world before they will let him out.

The excitement of a crowd, babbling in fourteen different languages, gave everyone the feeling that even a trip from Melbourne or Los Angeles, Tokyo or Helsinki had been worth it. Chairs and tables were arranged in a horseshoe pattern. The hall occasionally also serves not only as a theatre or cinema but also as a synagogue. The ark with its Torah scrolls was curtained off, wisely, to separate the holy words from the profane language of the Messiah.

There was a fifteen-minute delay before the presentation was to begin. Etan asked me how I was doing. I briefly mentioned to him my idea. He dismissed it with a quick gesture of his hand and asked after you. I told him of your predicament. He said we would meet Kohnstamm later. All Etan wanted to talk about was Elim, the celebrity, and how I met him in Iceland. I doubt if he believed a word of what I said.

Elim the Messiah is under house arrest in one of his own luxurious apartments on the first floor. The police had wanted to put him in jail or deport him to Belgium, but, because of his double nationality, Belgian and Israeli, and because deportation is a long drawn-out legal process, particularly when money to hire an entire army of lawyers is no object, they have dropped the idea. It's the hiring of an army of mercenaries which got him into this fix in the first place. Counter-Intelligence recently uncovered a sensational new terrorist outfit by the codename of 'Swift'. Truckloads of dynamite were about to enter Damascus, Teheran and Tripoli, the capitals of the three 'confrontation' states, driven by Palestinian suicide squads of two men each. For each separate operation twenty thousand dollars had been deposited in a secret Swiss bank account on behalf of the dependants. The trucks were to be detonated in the middle of the heaviest traffic, so as to cause the maximum havoc amongst pedestrians, motorists and adjacent buildings. A mad-hatter scheme that could have caused even more irreparable damage by backfiring at Israeli, American and European interests around the world.

The leader of the operation which was codenamed 'Springfield Market' was to be a professional terrorist, who would be totally unsuspected of having a hand in this: the world-famous Yossip Stalin Marcos, bought for fifty thousand either dollars or pounds (I forget which). The brain and financier behind all this I could hardly recognize when he entered the hall with bouncing steps and acknowledged the hush and tension with a wide grin. Could it possibly be the same man? The same slightly stooped forward, asthmatic man from Iceland? Either he must have spent the last few months at Tyringham health spa or the food at the Herzweg contains the same minimum of calories as the lemon juice-and-crackers menu they now serve in the renowned British clinic. He looked trim, even slim, his eyes sparkled. Instead of the grey flannel three-piece suit he wore in Reykjavik and Berlin, he was now dressed in white trousers, a smart white shirt and light-coloured perforated summer shoes. He could have been mistaken for a tennis star at Wimbledon, looked a good twenty years younger, seemed in radiant spirits and shook hands with friends in the first row. In a way I hoped he wouldn't spot me but he did.

'How was Amsterdam?' he said. 'You owe me a letter, remember?' I introduced him to Etan, who seemed duly impressed, so much so, in fact, that I gained new hope for myself. The Messiah sat down behind a small table covered with green baize cloth.

A few minutes later Kohnstamm strode in. A bulky man, about six foot two, with balding forehead and silvery mane. His eyes are ultramarine, grey with heavy bags under them. A large well-shaped mouth, splendid white teeth, probably as false as the man himself. The heavyweight champion among European Intellectuals, he claims to have been Freud's last student and one of his 'young friends'. He claims to have driven the Master to Aspang airport and to have seen him take off on his final journey to London. Kohnstamm is clearly another last pretender to the Freudian crown. He is the prototype of the self-assured Central European professor but suntanned, healthy and outgoing, like a Californian. The two together looked like a pair of ageing sportsmen. Next to the very tall Kohnstamm, Elim seemd small and even slim.

After a brief hush and a clearing of many throats Kohnstamm introduced his patient 'as the benefactor with a golden heart, who of his own accord has chosen to stay in his very own home in Jerusalem, which is thus honoured by his illustrious presence'. He called him 'a man of rare genius, a man of foresight, whose name is probably wrongly associated with a certain outrageous terrorist operation that never took place and is anyway too classified to be discussed in public', but did not get very far with his slippery speech.

'Bullshit! Liar! Cheat! Bum!' Elim screamed, to the delight of an audience gasping, coughing, and laughing. Meantime in his excitement Elim yelled even louder: 'Charlatan! Enemy agent!

Anti-Semite!' for additional effect. The spectacle was on.

Silence was finally restored. Elim rose. 'I am accused of sabotage, of anti-state activities, of trying to damage the security of this country and endanger the lives and property of its citizens. Nothing could be further from the truth. I have one aim and one aim only: the defence of this state and not its jeopardy, God forbid. To secure this state, the state must understand its role. It does not. One generation from now our children will enter the twenty-first century. Time marches on, but are the Zionists able to keep pace? Zionism may have helped us so far in the establishment of a state, but it is the political dream, the brainchild of a cultural provincialism of Czechs, Poles, Serbs and Hungarians – their separatist concepts after the downfall of the monarchy come true. Early Zionism modelled itself on these so-called Austro-Hungarian 'nationalists'. Their ideas are *passé* now, just like the ideas of the early communists, Fabian reformers and pre-war pacifists. All this is dead, all this is an unnecessary load of verbal garbage, and belongs on the dung heap of history. A modern 'state' demands twenty-first-century ideas. Our Zionist founding fathers led us out of one ghetto in Eastern Europe only to dump us in another ghetto in the Middle East ten times as forbidding as the one we left behind. A ghetto that once again preaches a ghetto mentality of subservience to our so-called powerful friends. These powers might or might not protect us when the next pogrom is due. But I say, and you can hear me loud and clear – even in the back row, I hope –' [he shouted at the top of his voice] ' – as the most progressive and most advanced nation in the area, we are equally entitled to call the tune in other capitals of the Middle East! This is part of a process in the slow and gradual conversion of all mankind to worship the One and Universal and not specifically Jewish God. How can we, of all people, be like others if we don't behave like others? A great military power must assume the duty such power demands. From narrow national interest we have evolved to universal preponderance! A historical revolution takes shape, ladies and gentlemen, under God's arbiter, judge and leader, His Messiah, His messenger, Elim Ffinger, the man standing here and now before you, a humble servant of God.'

Imagine the uproar such words would have caused among a public inclined to like neither Jews nor Zionists, old or new. Fortunately, all this took place in a closed session of psychiatrists and others who were more interested in the case history of this particular man than in the exploitation of the mad slogans this kind of man hands to his enemies. He repeatedly called Zionism an Austro-Hungarian plot for colonizing an underdeveloped backward Turkish province, but he also made it clear that he was not in the camp of the ultra orthodox anti-Zionist fanatics who hate the Jewish State, and rejoice even with its enemies to forestall the messianic delivery of its people by the Zionists.

When Kohnstamm tried to regain some of his authority he was crudely shouted down by his 'honoured house guest'. Elim commanded Kohnstamm to shut up because he had more important things to say and hadn't yet finished. In one way he was correct. The audience had come to study the patient and not his physician. Nothing Kohnstamm had to say could outweigh the ranting of the Messiah.

'Our peace effort must, I repeat, be accomplished not just by the force of arms and the lure of our cultural institutions, our superior health service, our technological brilliance. Moreover now the Messiah has arrived, it is within his power to dismiss all past, pre-messianic Rabbinical teachings regarding the perennial question of who is and who is not a Jew. I herewith declare all Palestinians to be Jews! They are the remnants of our ancestors who were not deported to Rome, but stayed behind to guard our land against foreign invaders! Whether they now profess to believe in Mohammed's teachings or profess to worship the Rabbi from Nazareth makes not the slightest difference. They still are Jews. Muslim Jews and Christian Jews, but Jews. Pre-messianic confusion has prevented many among us from seeing the light on this issue and I repeat: our own Palestinians are our own Jews! How do I know that? My very own voice tells me what to say and we all know, as believers, that our own voice is not of our own but of His, the Almighty's, making. I hear His voice in fourteen different languages, and I know I'm speaking the truth with my own voice in His name.'

With this kind of madness going on do you still think it's so important whether you have a dog or cat in the house? At least it wouldn't talk like this madman. Here, ultimate, millenial questions are being discussed, nothing less. 'Holiness is the secret of all life and the essence of our teachings!'

'My enemies threaten me! And he who threatens life, any life, is my natural enemy. There can never be peace between us. My credo, my belief provokes him. He must try to destroy me if I can't kill him before he strikes at me because he is my sworn enemy and I am his.'

He argues like you with your wife's late dog. Kill or be killed. Either I'll kill you or you'll kill me. It's not surprising you are both locked up.

'Our enemies promise us peace if we give them what they want. But all they want is to denounce our unique belief in life's holiness! We shall not grant them this. We are bound to defend our beliefs, if necessary by preventative and bloody action! I dismissed our President, our Ministers of Police and both the Chief Rabbis this morning. I shall soon also fire this man next to me.'

He might have lost a lot of weight since Reykjavik and changed his looks from sloppy intellectual to tennis champion but he was still the same maniac – only much worse. Not surprising they want to see him locked up safely. Yet they can't put him in prison for fear that he might easily infect others. In my view he is far too crazy to share a cell with common criminals. He is even too insane for a mental home. He's lucky he owns his own. Who else would put up with this kind of maniac? No wonder I love the man – he is, let's say, 'different'.

What a Catharsis, to meet a man at once more radical than

General Sharon and Rabbi Kahane put together, to show the world that we are a 'normal' nation at last and not the spittoon of other nations, as we have been accustomed to being. I only wish other people would follow our example and lock up their chauvinist troublemakers and let them talk freely, instead of making them presidents or heads of state with the power to put others away, or even kill them.

You have nothing to worry about. At lunch at the staff canteen Etan introduced me to Viktor Kohnstamm. He confirmed the man in charge of you is his nephew Bernard. He'll write to him and ask for your file or will simply telephone him. He was about to phone him anyway. He will suggest to revise your case immediately!

'Compared with what you heard this morning,' Kohnstamm grinned, 'your brother and his dog phobia is not too serious, don't you agree? What has happened to his wife?'

That's what I wanted to ask you, too. What has happened to Oksana? Where is she?

Yours, M.

## Letter from Oksana Borovsky
## to her brother-in-law Emmanuel
## Borovsky

The Lodge
Bishop's Avenue
London
3rd August

You may have heard the news, dear brother of Boris! My Boris is having analysis. He talks to the director and the director lets him talk. He lets him talk for an hour or two at a time, and sometimes four times a week. True, Boris has not many people to talk to where he is now. The inmates are not all intellectuals, like my dear Boris, there are a lot of businessmen, rich stockbrokers, a few politicians, a prince or two, these kind of people. 'The Country Club' Boris calls it, but no one he can have a good conversation with, the way he likes talking to you about God and the world. That's why he talks to the director now. A man with a nose as wide as an elephant's trunk and not much shorter either.

He is no beauty this doctor. But he is clever, my Boris says. I don't see it – but then I don't talk to him either. After I look at him for two seconds I feel sick. It's not just the nose. How can a man have been born with such lips? His lower lip hangs out like a piece of red jelly and his top lip is more like a leech, bloated and red. The eyes are equally disgusting. One looks to the right, one to the left, sometimes he rolls them in all directions. He has no eyebrows and no eyelashes, they are just thin yellow fluff, so to me he looks like a salamander – one of those chameleon-salamanders. You see them in the London Zoo.

Boris says he is not beautiful but very clever, and it's none of my business if he wants to talk to him. He says he charges him a special low rate, only seventy-five pounds an hour, and that's because you know his uncle and the uncle keeps on asking about Boris every time he phones from Jerusalem. A special price! Money is not his problem: the problem is how to convince Boris that he doesn't need all this nonsense.

The reason I am writing to you and begging you is: please write to my Boris – he listens to you – to stop telling everyone about our private affairs. Can you imagine! He talks to his director and tells him *everything*, everything we ever discussed, even what we did in private and how we did it. Everything. This is indiscretion, but he calls it analysis. Whenever I ask him what he says in his sessions, he avoids the topic. The first two times he told me but then he fell quiet, because he saw how much it upset me to have everyone, especially this ugly man, see me in the nude. He even gives him details about my most private parts, tells the doctor exactly what I say, when I sigh and all the rest of it.

You call this analysis? I call it treason. Betrayal. And I'll have to talk to Greenwald, my lawyer, and ask whether he is by law allowed to do what he is doing. Before I see my lawyer, please, Emmanuel, try to influence him and tell him to stop, before I take legal action.

Now to the second part of my letter: When I read him yours he became more pale every second, had to lie down and I had to fetch water for him. He passed out, then fell asleep. One, two. Just like that. I am convinced: my poor man is finished. Goodbye! Any second now he is going to sleep with his fathers. (That's what Boris calls dying.) Sleep with his fathers? My dear Boris snores like a rhinoceros. He doesn't believe me when I say, 'You are waking up the dead with the noise you make.' This time it looked like this was about to come true. After five minutes I wake him up. He had not been dead, fortunately, only very deep down in his sleep. When he suddenly realized he was alive, you know what he says first thing: 'It's all your fault.

Why read me this letter? Do you understand what has happened to Manny?'

I say: 'I understand he is in Jerusalem in a madhouse but as a visitor.' Maybe I shouldn't have said that, because this probably was another sore point with him when he realized you can come and go to and from the clinic in Jerusalem as you please, while he feels he is in prison here. Anyway, Boris shouts: 'My brother has converted! He is no longer a Jew!'

'Borishku,' I said to him, 'what are you saying? Where did you read in his letter that he has converted? There is not one line in the letter that says your brother has converted! Converted to what?' You know how Boris loves to make drama.

'Look at him!' he shouts, 'look at him! I met dozens of false Messiahs in my life, he meets his first one and what does he do? He instantly loses our religion.'

'What are you talking about, Borishku?'

'Our religion is to have faith in the real Messiah, the one who is still to come. What else is our religion if not belief in redemption to come?'

I know not enough about our religion, anyway, it's more his and yours than mine, to argue with him on such things.

'Even to go and listen to someone who claims to have come to save the world is blasphemy, better such a man were born deaf and blind!'

That's my Boris. Always making mountains out of molehills. He really is sick in his head and I'm glad he is safe in this house, where he is being looked after. When he comes out of here he still will never again be the same man. Eating, sleeping, walking in the park, sitting around in deck chairs and reading books and newspapers, making love to his Oksana – all this is past now. When he killed poor little Josh your brother committed suicide. His body is still moving about, but he killed his own soul. His soul, yes, his soul. His soul and my love are the same. A little of this love I gave to a sweet little dog. He goes and kills the dog. Therefore his soul must also be dead. Just look at his eyes! He

119

looks like a zombie now. It's not a happy ending to a wonderful love story, but that's how it sometimes ends.

Yours, Oksana

PS With all that going on I'm still a lucky woman. I have Walter who loves me. His flowers for me are his way of saying what's in his heart. I feel it. He loves me too much to admit it. That's why he always tells stupid jokes: 'I buy at fourteen and sell at twenty,' this kind of stupid remark. I am not twenty, not thirty, but nearly forty. At my age a woman knows her blossoms have fallen long ago. But a man who loves blossoms sooner or later gets also to harvest the ripe fruit. Once he tastes the ripe, mature sweet fruit, he knows what's what and that there is nothing better to come. The summer spells the end. That's why grown-up mature women frighten grown-up mature men and even not-so mature men. Don't ask me why. When a man reaches an age to enjoy an older woman, he is afraid, afraid of his mortality. He knows in his heart there is no mercy before Him who makes the laws of nature. If you can't fight death all you can fight is your fellow man. That's why there will always be fighting, every man against every man – until all will be dead. And they'll always blame us women for their stupidity. Of course. What else?

Meanwhile Walter keeps sending me roses: more and more roses arrive every week. The old ones are still fresh when a new bunch arrives. He is burying me under roses, the old pervert. Their perfume is so strong I have trouble breathing at night and have to put them outside the room I sleep in. Walter loves me, true. And I too love him, though not the same way as I love my Boris, because the bastard, your brother, killed my little dog, my love, and with this nearly killed me, maybe even did. Anyway I love him more. I only wish he wouldn't discuss his intimate life with an elephant. Please tell him that next time you write to him.

O.

# Letter from Emmanuel Borovsky
## to his brother Boris

Hotel King David
Jerusalem
9th August

I am still saddened by your letter of the 12th. I wish I could help you with the English weather. As far as I know there is only one man in the world, a certain Laurel Bruce Pierce II of Burbank, California, who claims he has ways and means of changing the English weather. 'It'll stop raining in your country,' he told a British journalist who came to interview him, 'when the people of Britain also look more sunny and cheerful. It's the people, after all, who make their own weather and not the other way round.' He should know. He is one of those Californians with a reputation for having prevented several earthquakes in southern California by meditation and creating positive energy in such enormous quantities, it also changed a drought that was threatening the lettuce farmers of La Jolla into two weeks of rainstorms (after he had collected a modest twenty-five thousand dollars for his spirited efforts).

Alas, the man overdid it and was practically lynched. The rainstorms not only destroyed the lettuce crops, they also devastated the tomatoes, cucumbers and radishes over an area of fifty square miles. Laurel Bruce Pierce offered his 'positive energy' services to the British public, for a fee, but found no buyers. I read all this in the *Herald Tribune* and wouldn't swear to it. Still seems he is the only man who may be able to halt the summer rains in Essex.

Here the sun shines so constantly that not just the inmates of the Herzweg (I visit Elim now practically every day), but also the staff drag their feet because of the heat wave. You should hear Elim shout and rant when he has to wait an hour for his breakfast. Now Kohnstamm has left for Aswan and Cairo for a holiday (not before posting two armed guards in the grounds, in case his illustrious house guest tries one of his Houdini Tricks). Elim is the boss here, but he is not allowed to leave the Herzweg until the President grants him amnesty. He is 'confined at Her Majesty's pleasure' they call it in England.

Elim, as you may expect, not only treats the staff like his personal servants, he addresses his fellow inmates, too, as if they were 'his' patients, which they are in a way. He does own the place, after all. He gave me a list of 'his' current 'house guests'. What a cast of characters! Another Saviour, a Maronite Christian from Beirut, a small tight-lipped mousy fellow, no competition to Elim. There are two Kings of Israel. One a dentist from Natanya called David Sternovsky, the other an ice-cream vendor from Tiberias, who holds court dressed in a toga with a crown made of junk jewellery. His name is Simchah Mizrachi and every Saturday he is visited by his extended family clan and they all have a noisy picnic on the lawn in front of my window. When the noise gets too much, Elim appears like a camp commandant and orders everyone to leave his house instantly. You can imagine what happens: the noise gets ten times louder and no one leaves until it's time to go before it gets dark.

Right now we have three Jehovahs in the house but only one Jesus. Two of the Jehovahs are Presbyterian Missionaries from New Zealand (twin brothers), the third one, a handsome young engineer from Bucharest. Our Jesus is a Portuguese deck hand who actually calls himself Paolo Jesus Junior and claims to be the illegitimate son of Ben Gurion and Golda Meir. He can't explain his odd parentage he told me, but is ready to walk up to Golgotha and be nailed to a cross if he were allowed out. That should prove it.

Yes, there is one other Jesus, but he calls himself 'the one and only true *Christian* Jesus' because he is not circumcised (yet Jewish on both his parents' sides). He is a pitiful hunchback born in Tel Aviv and wasn't circumcised because his parents had not decided whether to stay in the country or go back to Lyon, from where they had emigrated in 1949.

We have a Satan called Berl Popovsky, who really is a poor devil. He has the round eyes and stunted growth of the mongoloid and all he can shout is 'Satan, Satan, I am the Satan!' What a nebbish!

We have quite a large-sized non-Jewish contingent of Holy Ghosts – French, English and Dutch – among them a neat fifty-five-year-old Lutheran lady born in Hanover called Teresa Kurzschluss. I could go on and tell you the story of everyone here but what's the point? You have your own interesting cast of characters, I am sure. Maybe I am only speaking for myself; but I rather enjoy this community of so-called disturbed people for a number of reasons. Chief among them: the honesty and sincerity and the simplicity of heart everyone shows. I have time to lie around, think and rest and write. The kitchen is run by one of the best 'French Chefs' in the Middle East, a marvellous enormous Italian, obese and disgusting-looking, who takes it as a compliment when people complain of being overweight, which practically everyone here is, except Elim, who lives on pomegranates and yoghurt. I hope this finds you in good health.

Yours, M.

## Letter from Boris
## to Emmanuel Borovsky

Old King's Hall
Chelmsford
Essex
17th August

No I am not dead, not yet dearest brother, just that I have said goodbye to some of my previous conceptions about myself. From what I gather from your letter you have given up the idea of building a machine for accelerated redemption. I suppose you couldn't raise the money for the research. Maybe it's all to the good. I can't tell, I am no longer interested in God and the world, as I used to be, though I still get angry if I detect defection and betrayal of our religion, and it hurts in particular when this happens so close in the family. But what can I do? For the first time in my life, I am thinking about my own mind and trying to save my soul. To save yourself and not the whole world at the same time is not necessarily against our religion.

Bernard Kohnstamm, our director, has become my analyst. The inmates here call him 'Dr Barmy' or 'Dr Crazy'. But he is far from crazy. Yesterday he said to me: 'You know Mr Boris, I believe you have the excremental vision. You see excrement everywhere. But let it not upset you. Jonathan Swift suffered the same delusions. He too had the excremental vision. Remember his YAHOO?'

In the library they have all of Jonathan Swift's collected works. The more I read about the yahoo the more I begin to understand my own life and my own tragedy. 'The yahoo is endowed with a very ranky smell, somewhat between a weasel and a fox, which, heightened at mating time, is a positive attraction to the male of the species.' This recognition of the rank odour stayed with Gulliver even after his return to England, and he confides: 'During the first year I could not endure my wife or children in my presence, the very smell of them was intolerable . . . when I walked the street I kept my nose stopped with rue, lavender or tobacco leaves.' (That should explain our love for cigarettes and other tobacco products!)

The yahoo's eating habits are not less filthy: 'There was nothing that rendered the yahoos more odious than their undistinguished appetite to devour everything that came in their way, whether herbs, roots, berries, corrupted flesh of animals or all mingled together.' It sounds all too familiar.

But more than anything the yahoos distinguish themselves from other animals by their attitude towards their own excrement. 'The essence of Swift's vision and Gulliver's redemption is the recognition that civilized man not only remains a yahoo but is worse than a yahoo. And the essence of yahoo is filthiness, a filthiness *that does not distinguish a yahoo from our civilized citizens but only from other animals,*' (says Norman Brown on Swift's behalf).

Quintana called it 'crude sensationalism' and Middleton Murry, who suffered the pangs of modern barbarism, was shocked and outraged: 'For even if we carry the process of stripping the human to the limit of imaginative possibility we do not arrive at the yahoo. We might arrive at his cruelty and malice but we should never arrive at this nastiness and filth. . . . A gratuitous degradation of humanity, not a salutary but a shocking one,' complains Middleton Murry feebly.

Three years in German labour camps and one year in Siberia, or a few years among Polish partisans, is all the shock therapy our generation needed to immunize us against the squeamishness of Swift's critics. The filthy yahoo habits haven't changed either because there is now relative peace (instead of a world war going on). I sublimated my disgust, my nausea by hating dogs and cats instead of doing the healthy thing and simply hating my fellow men, or just: people. Kohnstamm helps me and so does reading Jonathan Swift. It analyses and explains the motives that got me here in the first place. Yet to be honest, I'd rather sublimate my hatred by hating dogs than confront the stench in the world. You mentioned that in Vienna they call it the *Foehn*, but men's filthy habits are everywhere and globally evident.

Despite all my misgivings: maybe it's better to chase a phantom Messiah than a stupid harmless dog? Whichever way I look at it: I envy you for your enterprising spirits. I remember you've always been like that. 'Inventing' was in your blood, ever since you were a toddler. You were only three and I was five but I'll never forget how you shrieked, laughed and danced like a little Indian, howling with delight. The reason for all this spectacle? You had just, I believe it must have been for the first time, identified yourself in a mirror! I wish I had been that happy when I discovered myself. You were instantly happy with yourself, must have believed you had caused, 'made' yourself, come true. What imagination! Or is this just my conjecture? My own fantasy?

Yours, Boris

# Letter from Emmanuel Borovsky
# to his brother Boris

The Herzweg House
Jerusalem
22nd August

To paraphrase Descartes: 'It stinks, therefore I am' and why not?

Watch out with analysis. All sorts of things might crop up. Analysis, like submarine archaeology, could bring to light all sorts of horrors you might prefer to have left buried deep down below. I still have only one explanation for why you are afraid of hating people and sublimate it by hating dogs. If you show your hatred for people, you may provoke their own fears and subsequent aggression. You are, let's face it, afraid to hate people, whether or not their fragrance is acceptable to you. You obviously are a coward and to be a coward shows you have a strong sense of self-preservation, which is normal.

I have another explanation of why you shot the dog. It goes like this: the dog had a male name and you regarded the animal subconsciously as your offspring. Subconsciously, again, you had fathered a monster. Oksana 'gave' you a dog instead of a son. How could anyone accept such a 'gift'? You had to get rid of it: there was no way around the inevitable. Josh Brown's death served another purpose. He was the second man, the other man in the house. By killing your rival you proved to Oksana the sincerity of your love and devotion for her. How do you like that? If you'd read the letter she wrote to me you'd know (but you know that anyway) that she loves you now more than ever. Naturally. You 'won' her and she is now all yours. She really is devoted to you. That's why I am taking the liberty of reminding you that you upset her very much by telling your analyst what she looks and feels like in bed. I am sure she has told you that as well, but she also asked me to remind you how much she loathes to be 'exposed'. You and I know she is not squeamish or shy, she just thinks your director is extremely ugly, and she doesn't feel like being undressed in front of an ugly man. You can't fault her for that! Excuse this invasion of your privacy, but Oksana begged me specially to write to you about it. She seems more convinced than I am you'll listen to me.

Yours, M.

PS I presume you won't mind if I point out that your breakdown was much overdue. All those years of work and achievements are bound to take their toll, particularly when we begin to relax, when we think we can now settle down. Like retirement at a late age, it's fraught with danger. If you had decided to retire at a young age, like me, before success spoiled you rotten, you wouldn't have had to go through this crisis. If you had fallen in love with a woman your age or older you wouldn't be in such a spin, either. You'd have lost your obsession with her body after a brief spell of exploration. In less than two weeks you might have been 'cured'. That's not always the case, but it's a strong possibility we can't discount.

# Letter from Boris Borovsky
# to his brother Emmanuel

Old King's Hall
Chelmsford
Essex
29th August

You no-good bastard! Why do you let me down? All this
smooth moralizing and analysing and not a word about when
you are coming to see me. What have I done to deserve this?
Why this uncalled-for cruelty? Why aren't you a brother and
friend in need? The entire universe needs your redemption, yes
of course, but your own brother may get lost in the labyrinth of
his own mind and you don't care a fart. Whether or not Oksana
loves me now more than ever is not to the point. She has me in
her power anyway and totally. She has thrown me into a well,
dumped me in this dungeon, chained me to her whims,
branded me with hot irons of ridicule mingled with pity. I'll
soon lose my last bit of hope and I'll die, yes I'll die here the way
I never believed it could happen. Alone and forgotten by those
closest to me.

Yours, etc.

# Letter from Emmanuel
## to Boris Borovsky

The Herzweg House
Jerusalem
8th September

I don't recognize you. Have you really gone mad? Just because you happen to be confined in a lunatic asylum, that's no reason to lose all your self-control. You killed a dog – so what? You mistook him for Oksana's lover and also for your own miscreant of an offspring. Those things happen. Enough of this self-pity! And what's all this madness with 'excremental vision'? Old hat. Swift copied it from the Ecclesiastes: 'All is vanity and vexation of spirit and there is no profit under the sun.' Well isn't that true? The excremental vision has only helped us to see things clearer. That's what you get from paying attention to the literary genius of Swift. He confuses you with words. You would do better to listen to charlatans, maniacs and madmen, as I do. Wisdom hides in their madness like strains of pure gold buried in sand. If he has solved no one else's problems, Elim certainly solved all mine. More or less. Compared to him I have no more obsession with Jews and redemption of the world. I feel a free man, for the first time in my life. Thank God for sending me my Messiah!

Elim has arranged a two-bedroomed apartment for me, furnished with taste and money, next to his. Full board included. All for free. Not quite free, of course. I have to listen to his idiocies, but I do it while we play chess. So that's fine. Playing chess with the 'Messiah' in the heart of Jerusalem, the spiritual capital of the Western world, is a fate I can endure. I have time to write. I can come and go as I please. I don't pay the King David's outrageous rents, and the food here is prepared for gourmets, not for American tourists. You eat like a *mensch* and live like a *mensch* here, and when I'm fed up with this kind of existence I'll move on. From Inventor I have progressed to Messiah's Consultant. Frankly I have not a care in the world and no sexual problem either. It is not just the Holy City: the entire country is full of beautiful over-sexed women, no more than a phone call away. I've found my Redeemer, I'm fine. And he is always entertaining. Today at lunch (if I told you the menu, your mouth would water, too cruel, that's why I'd better not tell you) we discussed another plot. The conversion of Hirohito, the Emperor. Once this is accomplished with the help of a Japanese Rabbi, who has been working on the idea for years, we'll have two hundred million more (Japanese) Jews. If the King of the Khazars could do it in the ninth century, why not repeat the same? Yes, why not indeed? I told him, when he asked me what I thought of it, that it was a grandiose idea and we should go right ahead with it. Irving Cohen and his influence on the Spanish Court were a mere figment of my imagination. This man Elim Ffinger is for real!

Tuesday
Kohnstamm is back and avoids both of us most of the time but occasionally he *kibitzes* over our game. Most of the moves he suggests are shrewd but Elim is definitely the better player of the two of them. And me? I play to lose. It's a trick to encourage his over-confidence. One day I'll strike and beat him. Don't you think that's clever strategy?

Yours, M.

# Letter from Boris
## to his brother Emmanuel Borovsky

Old King's Hall
Chelmsford
Essex
19th September

Dear Manny,

Don't believe I'll let you get away with it even though you too seem to be a victim. Madness may afflict all of us when we least expect it. Shadows simply jump out of the dark and strike you down. Suddenly. What petty criminals do to the man who walks down the street minding his own business, the Almighty does to us too with an invisible hand. He blesses you with His right and suddenly floors you with His left. He blessed me with wealth and comfort, brains and good health and then sent me a demon to torture my soul. He could have postponed whatever I deserve till the next life but here He shows His scepticism. He knows about temporality and punishes us in the Here and Now. Good God He is. 'Later will be what will be' as the Gorali in the Tatra Mountains, where our father was born, used to say.

He gave me a devil for a wife and an egomaniac for a beloved brother. I can't argue with Him. Who can? But I can argue with you. I resent your way of treating me, your brother whom you love, with such coldness. 'Of course we never stop loving our own flesh and blood,' you'll say, 'though it may seem so at times.' I know your yarn. Do you think I shall leave you to your new friend so he may have your sick soul under his control forever? I am not *that* mad, I assure you. Nor do I believe you 'have no choice' but to stay with him because he foots the bills.

Not to beat about the bush, I, too, over the year have kept you in reasonable comfort. I could afford it and did it with love, as you know, despite the fact that you constantly squander money and never save, as matter of principle, it seems.

To the point: I insist that you come here and see me, spend time with me before you decide to take up permanent residence in Jerusalem. If you really want to be in an asylum I am sure we'd find you a place here at the Old King's Hall. There are many empty rooms and suites on the top floor, as the prices went up steeply at the beginning of the year. Many wealthy people can no longer afford it here and have to stay at home with their families unless they can use their madness professionally and become politicians or professional patriots. Madness has never stopped and will never hinder an ambitious man's career, on the contrary it has furthered it more often than not, as we well know.

I want you to be with me and suffer me for a while. I want you, too, to get drenched by the constant rains. Your brother is also an egoist, also a self-centred fool, just like you, or I wouldn't insist, that's obvious. Yes I am a fool, a narcissist, a pitiful creature, I know it and I admit to it. Still I am your brother and your place is here, by me, at least for a while. Leave the eternal Jerusalem and come to a temporary exile and you'll be out of earshot of your 'Redeemer' and his redemption scenarios. This in itself can only be to the good: it certainly can't harm you to get away from him and it will help me to have you here by my side. You'll be a truly free man!

I beseech you once more. I beg you and I demand. Take the next plane to Heathrow, a train to Chelmsford and a taxi from the railway station and you can be here within the next twenty-four hours. You will of course remember the place. Your memory might have suffered a little but you can't have forgotten everything. Wire me when to expect you and I'll send my chauffeur with the Bentley to collect you from the airport. Have a safe flight,

Your loving
brother, B.

PS If you are short of money say so. British Airways in Jerusalem will have a ticket waiting for you. Just say the word.

# From Emmanuel Borovsky
## to his brother Boris

The Herzweg House
Jerusalem
21st September

Dearest brother,
Love is no empty phrase in my heart. You know it, I know it.
It's not a word one mentions when one knows it exists. We
don't lack love between us, just understanding. We must try to
understand one another better.

How, I ask myself, can I really help you? Hold your hand?
Kiss your brow? Stroke your hair? That's what Oksana is for.
From what I gather you two are as close, if not closer, as you
ever were, except that you no longer share the same bed. Josh
Brown, a humble creature, a dog, came between you two. He
might be dead now but so is your love life. To return to the land
of the living you must accept and follow my advice.

You must pay lawyers and psychiatrists anything they want
to cheat and lie on your behalf, and pay them so well they won't
mind a little trouble with the law, should it come to that. After
all, that's what money is for. To bribe, to buy and to redeem is
money's true value. I have had time to meditate about it:
redemption needs cash, not an electronic flash. Redemption?
What does it mean to you, ask yourself . . . You have the money,
the cash to buy yourself freedom but you are unfit to know
what to do with it. That's what subjugation and slavery is all
about: either the lack of the filthy lucre or the incapacity to
enjoy freedom. You are a serf and that's why I refuse to see you.

A man who has lost his mind for the love of a woman, lost his mind. He cannot be redeemed, he is lost and sunk.

Don't compare our situations. I can come and go as I please here, I am here of my own free will. And I don't love the man who pulled me in here, as a matter of fact I hate him more than I'd like to admit, but . . . I repeat, I'm here voluntarily. If I feel like it I'll leave here tomorrow and I might. I may go back to the Alligator Island and to Australia Mallone for a while or forever, or come and go and do whatever I please. I am a free bird in the wild. Call me a *luftmensch*, I don't mind. And I don't need an Oksana, a passionate, foolish, childish love, to suffer. I have learned to endure the excrements, the shit in this world (as you'd call it) without this kind of love. 'Whoever thinks he is suffering hasn't suffered enough,' said the *Übermensch* on Nietzsche's behalf. Get out of your cage, smile again and change the British weather and I'll be with you in no time. I am your brother and am just as self-centred as you. Here the sun doesn't cease to shine and you could join the two of us, Elim and me plotting the takeover of the world.

Fantastic? Mad? Outrageous? Besotted? No, brother, I have become very realistic, I am a realist – at last.

Yours, M.

# Letter from Boris Borovsky
# to his brother Emmanuel

Brown's Hotel
Dover Street
London W1
22nd October

You haven't heard from me for a while and this for a number of good reasons. For a month or so I was so furious with you, so angry I couldn't write. You had torn me to shreds by calling me, correctly, a slave. All my life I had thought I was a free man and then it began to dawn on me that you were right. I had dispatched my canine rival to hell and wrapped his leash around my own neck just like the submissive creature I was and handed my Mistress the chain to pull or relax, depending on her mood. Then one day I woke up and told Oksana I had rung Martin my lawyer, because I wanted a divorce.

Two days later Martin came and we settled everything with Oksana, amicably. Of course she cried a lot and I suppose she'll go on crying for much, much longer, until she stops. I left her The Lodge and the Bentley to cry in. With the money we deposited for her she can purchase a zoo.

There is a time for everything and I had simply reached the point when I had had enough of her. As I said: I woke up.

For the moment I'm staying at Brown's Hotel but I have made arrangements to visit you in Jerusalem. We could spend a week or so together and the three of us could hatch quite a few nice plots for how to run the world. The more I think about it the more I begin to understand God's mystical intentions to have the affairs of men ruled by men who are more than qualified for such high office, not in spite of but *because* they are considered crazy, abnormal, demented by a majority which considers itself to be sober, normal and in control of all its faculties. What a great triumvirate we would make!

'The stone that the builders rejected became the corner-stone,' it says somewhere in the Old Book in classical cryptic code.

Let me please know by return when it's convenient and you shall soon see me in Jerusalem. I have made a tentative booking at the King David as I don't expect you can or want to put me up. I see no need for that much proximity anyway. I am grateful to you, dearest brother; you reminded me what to do with my money. Instead of building myself a prison to buy myself free.

I must say here: Martin also was most helpful. He would have arranged everything for half the fee but I insisted he take a hundred thousand to ease me out of my burden. After some heated arguments he accepted and the rest went smoothly. Twenty-four hours later I was home again, packed a single suitcase and took a taxi to Brown's Hotel. Why I chose a hotel with the same name as my late rival is something I refuse to unravel. It's sheer coincidence, I assure you. Claridges and the Mayflower, the Westbury and the Connaught were all booked up because there is a convention of former OPEC members in town. Please write to me by return at the above address.

Yours, Boris

# Letter from Emmanuel
## to his brother Boris Borovsky

Hotel Palace
Coopers Town
Grand Cayman Island
26th November

What a homecoming I had, dearest Boris. Australia brought her entire family, all twenty-seven of them, and the drinking, eating and feasting went on until dawn. How I love these people here! I can't describe it and I can't explain why. I can only guess and my guess is because they are totally alien to me and our past. How can I convey to you how marvellous it is to communicate with people who never heard of Poland and Germany, of Auschwitz and Austria, of Jews and goyim, of the old anti-Semitism from the right and the current one from the left. The words redemption, Sabbtai Zvi and Social Justice as a result of electronic engineering exist for them maybe in books and of course they don't read here.

What they know about our people, the Jews, is what the priest of their Church of the 'Twelfth House of Israel' tells them: ie, the Blacks are the true descendants of the Queen of Sheba and King Solomon and therefore the true and only real Jews in the world. The Messiah too, either in his First or Second Coming, is going to be a black (what else?) and will rule the world from Addis Ababa and this quite soon! Quite soon means after the restoration of the Monarchy in Ethiopia, after the heirs of the Lion of Judah, the Emperor Haile Selassi, are allowed to return from their exile in Khartoum, Cairo, London,

Paris and New York. Thank God, their real Messiah, like ours, is in no hurry either apparently.

Elim left Jerusalem after I left. He was let out on parole and deported to Belgium. As we don't correspond I can't tell you what he is up to at the moment. But should you by chance hear or read anywhere that the Chief Rabbi of Paris is dining secretly on roast pork; that the Archbishop of Paris *Monseigneur* Lustiger, who was born a Jew, still puts on his *tfillim* when saying his morning prayers in the privacy of his bathroom; that Khaddaffy is an agent on the payroll of the Mossad and CIA; or that Margaret Thatcher is a secret follower of the Rebbe, the Lubavitscher of course, wears a wig, lights candles Friday night, regularly takes the ritual bath, and occasionally travels incognito to Brooklyn to visit her Master at his court – you'll know right away where this kind of rumour originates. These stories will have been planted in the world press by my former employer, the Messiah from Antwerp, who no longer asks for or needs my advice or yours.

Yours, M.